Dangerous Neighbors

A NOVEL BY

BETH KEPHART

LAURA GERINGER BOOKS

EGMONT
USA
NEW YORK

EGMONT
We bring stories to life

First published by Egmont USA/Laura Geringer Books, 2010
443 Park Avenue South, Suite 806
New York, NY 10016

1 3 5 7 9 8 6 4 2

www.egmontusa.com
www.beth-kephart.blogspot.com

Library of Congress Cataloging-in-Publication Data

Kephart, Beth.
Dangerous neighbors / Beth Kephart.
p. cm.
Summary: Set against the backdrop of the 1876 Centennial Exhibition in Philadelphia, Katherine cannot forgive herself when her beloved twin sister dies, and she feels that her only course of action is to follow suit.
ISBN 978-1-60684-080-1 (hardcover) —
978-1-60684-106-8 (reinforced library binding)
[1. Twins—Fiction. 2. Sisters—Fiction. 3. Death—Fiction. 4. Grief—Fiction. 5. Guilt—Fiction. 6. Centennial Exhibition (1876 : Philadelphia, Pa.)—Fiction. 7. Philadelphia (Pa.)—History—19th century—Fiction.] I. Title.
PZ7.K438Dan 2010
[Fic]—dc22
2010011249

Printed in the United States of America

CPSIA tracking label information:
Random House Production • 1745 Broadway • New York, NY 10019

For
Laura Geringer.

Because.

Dangerous Neighbors

It is 1876, the height of the Centennial Exhibition in Philadelphia. Katherine has lost her twin sister, Anna, and though it was an accident, Katherine remains convinced that Anna's death was her fault. One wickedly hot September day, Katherine sets out for the exhibition grounds to cut short the life she is no longer willing to live.

This is the story of what happens.

One

FROM UP HIGH, EVERYTHING SEEMS TO SPILL FROM ITSELF. Everything is shadowed. The cool at the base of trees. The swollen lip of river. The dark beneath the cliff stones at Rockland, where Katherine had gone last week—taken the steamer, hiked to the summit, and stayed until almost too late. "Oh, Katherine," her mother had sighed the next day, her hand on the door, the velvet streamers falling crooked from her hat, her eyes fixed on the mud on Katherine's skirt. "I wish you wouldn't."

"I know what you wish."

"I'm off to Mrs. Gillespie's."

"I know that, too."

Never enough sky. Never near enough to the scooped-out wings of the hawk. Katherine walks the ridge above the river or goes all the way to George's Hill and stands two hundred and ten feet above high tide—keeping her distance from the boys and their kites, the foreigners with their funny talk and funny way of climbing. Keeping her distance to find the courage for what will be, she has decided—her last escape. Because Anna, her twin, has died, and she had no business dying. Because Anna's body, once a mirror of Katherine's own, is in a cherrywood box dug deep into the side of Laurel Hill.

Don't let me get old, Katherine can almost hear Anna saying. And look: *Congratulations, Katherine! You have granted your sister her one ill-begotten wish.*

Katherine climbs and tells no one where she is. She's climbed through February and March, through April and May, June and July. Sometimes Katherine has left the house in a light wool dress with a scarf looped loose around her neck and then, of a sudden, the weather has changed. In has blown an infiltrating wind and there Katherine has stood on Belmont Plateau, all the way up, inside the cage of the Sawyer Observatory, securing the scarf around her chin. She has stood and stared out onto the coves and hollows of the Centennial park; the great copper dome of Saints Peter and Paul; the houses, theaters, banks set tight upon the city's checkerboard squares. She has studied the unfinished pile of City Hall—like a half-baked cake, she has thought, with too much buttercream. It has never mattered how fiercely the weather has blown: Katherine has remained up high, seeking reconciliation or redemption, and finding neither.

"Anna," Katherine says aloud, "how could you?"

At home, meanwhile, Katherine's mother and father have gone on living—climbing down the stairs in the morning and taking their places in the dining room, where the sun falls flat across the table and where Jeannie Bea, the cook, serves eggs and scrapple. She brings Katherine's father *The Public Ledger* and her mother the latest issue of *The New Century for Women.* Afterward Katherine's mother plucks an old straw hat from the hook on the back wall. She fixes the contraption on her head and trails back toward the kitchen to check her reflection in the bottom of Jeannie Bea's biggest copper pot. Then she steps through the hall and toward the front door, the whisper of her black overskirt fading to silence.

All the while Katherine's father folds and unfolds the pages of his *Ledger*, scanning the advertisements for news of missing mules and piano lessons, proposals for coal, the offer for sale of hoisting machines and dumbwaiters, all of which, he firmly believes, are economic measures, portents. Katherine's father has a mind for calculations. He has a knack for looking ahead and seeing the future, which is his job at the Philadelphia National Bank, but he had not looked ahead on behalf of Anna, and maybe Katherine will never forgive him for that. Maybe she will never forgive her mother either. Nor will her mother, preoccupied with tea and crackers, with women's rights and unrealized freedoms, speak of it. There was to be no investigation—that's what her mother had said. Katherine has slumped on the stoop of their house at night, waiting for her mother to come home from one of those inexorable ladies' meetings. She has stood outside her mother's bedroom door, afraid to knock. *Let me tell you what happened*, she has tried to say. *Blame me so that you might forgive me, so that I might forgive myself.*

But her mother has said, "What is gone now is gone." She is brisk, efficient above all. The future lies in the future, she says, and never in the past. Katherine knows now what will happen when she, too, dies young. Life, more or less, will go on.

Katherine roams. Sometimes heading for the dark cave of bones at the Academy of Natural Sciences, sometimes for the chess room at the Mercantile Library, where she watches the games without comment. But mostly Katherine goes to the highest places she can find; and today, her very final day, she chooses the Colosseum. She has a plan; she will fly and soon feel nothing.

The summer has been stifling, but today there is air, at least. Katherine is wearing navy blue—an improvement, her mother had said, and that was all her mother had said earlier that day, staring at her over Jeannie Bea's eggs at breakfast: "You're looking more your age now, Katherine. Blue isn't black; it's more becoming." Were Anna alive, she'd have rolled her eyes behind her hand and laughed at their mother talking about fashion. She'd have said, while they lay in bed that night, "And what color is Mother's dress, is Mother's *every* dress? Oh yes, I nearly forgot: she favors black."

They buried Anna in February when the ground was frozen. It took two men one week to ready the hole—to dig it out and shimmy it smooth. It was Katherine's father who held Katherine back when the cherrywood box went in—his arm around her waist, one hand on her shoulder. She'd have jumped in, fallen. She'd have taken her place beside her sister—her dress muddy at the hem. "Let her go now, my darling. Let her go." Her father's words in her disbelieving ear.

Into a hole in a hill? Inside a box?

In the weeks following the funeral, in the interminable months, Katherine would go to Laurel Hill—take the steamboat to the foot of the cliff and rise up under the inverted *U* of the stone bridge and wander through the city of the dead beneath the slight shade of the junipers and the obelisks, past the neighborhoods of mausoleums. It was marble against sky. It was the gleam of granite. It was the beginning or ending of rhododendron blooms, and always Katherine came bearing gifts. A single white tulip. A red silk string. The architecture of a robin's nest. As if it would be possible to return Anna to herself. Katherine would sit, talking to Anna, imploring Anna, making promises she could not keep, giving Anna the news of the house, the latest on Mother, and when the shadows shifted, Katherine would lie down, her head on the pillow of her hands. That's when Bennett would come. When she would open her eyes and see him cresting the hill or standing there by the scruff of roses. He would call out to her, saying, "Can't we talk?" and she would run—down past the stones, urns, vases, yews, past the cast iron and the sandstone, over the tangle of exposed roads, under the arch.

No, Bennett. We cannot talk. We will never *talk. I've nothing to tell you.*

But that is the past, behind her. Today is today, and Katherine hurries up Chestnut, past the banks, past the Custom House and Independence Hall. At Eighth Street she turns and heads south, then turns again, west onto Locust, until the Academy of Music is in sight. On her side of Broad Street is Kiralfy's Alhambra Palace—Moorish and tight, arched, a bright splash of white and color out of sync even with a city that has turned itself into a circus for the year.

From high above Broad, chimes announce the hour: four o'clock. In the street the horses twitch their ears toward the song; the chestnut vendors lift their chins. An old woman staggers to the street to get a view. Katherine waits until the traffic clears, then lifts her skirts and runs. By the time she reaches the arched entrance of the Colosseum, her lungs feel sucked of air.

She moves through the door, and pays. She turns and stands before the globular world of the cyclorama—"Paris by Night," the advertisements call it. Either the wide boulevards of that French city no longer live in Paris, or someone has, as all the papers promised, pulled off a masterly trick. There are the painted gaslights that seem to flicker. There is the streaming and surging of the Seine. There are the buildings projecting and receding, the shadows in doorways, the women talking, a cat asleep in an alley set to stir, and one man in particular, putting a flame to his pipe. "Paris by Night" has been canvased onto the round interior walls of the Colosseum, more alive than anything.

In the press of the strangers around her, Katherine is aware of a girl with dark hair at her elbow, taking the spectacle in and turning now to Katherine for some kind of an explanation, but Katherine hasn't time for that. "Your mama's that way," Katherine says, turning her shoulder like her mother might have done and walking toward the celestial sky, where it is night, and the moon is bright, and the stars can see.

"They didn't miss a detail, did they?" a stranger remarks. "Saves you the trouble of a long boat ride."

"I wouldn't mind the ride," Katherine murmurs.

"The sea is fine," declares the woman, "save in a storm."

An odd thing to say, except—no sooner has the stranger spoken than the whole Colosseum goes dark and a storm drives in, and now rain falls hard over Paris, torrents of it streaming down. Amid shouts of astonishment and applause, the rains still come, until gradually, soundlessly, the clouds rub off and the moon again shines high. The stranger is gone. Another child stands beside Katherine, a little boy dressed in a blue sailor suit, who calls for his father until his father comes and hoists him up onto his shoulders.

"It was raining," the boy tells his father.

"I know it was."

"It was raining and I didn't get wet."

"It's the age of miracles, son."

Beneath the moon and the stars, Paris is shining. The boulevards, the river, the haberdasheries, the windows of pastry shops, the streetlamps. At an open-air café, a couple dances, and at the far end of the widest boulevard a poodle at the end of its leash wags its tail. Katherine takes it all in, for here she is, spending her last day on earth in Paris, after a storm. It is more beauty than she bargained for. It hurts to think about all that goes on in the world that she has never known and will not now. It hurts that the real Paris is far away across the ocean and that she will never see it.

She takes her time. She finds her way to the Otis elevator and when the big doors slide open, she climbs in, rides the smug machine with the wild-eyed crowd all the way to the balconied tower, where there are yet more stairs to climb, views to be had, but there is also—Katherine has planned on this—a band of windows just above the thick drum of the cyclorama. The windows open easily onto the slanted roof. Where the roof completes itself there is a straight drop toward the hard scape of the city. Katherine has stood at Broad and Locust, looking up, calculating the distance. She has considered the unbending nature of the street. The smack of absolution.

The others climb high. Their voices disappear into the narrow channel above. Katherine bends down to retie her boots with excruciating deliberation, until at last she is alone with her plan—alone in this round room with its unlocked windows, with Paris below and the balconies above. She moves with the utmost care—one leg through the nearest window and then the other, both hands steady on the wooden frame. A splinter catches in one finger. Her feet adjust to the mathematics of the roof. She turns to face the sky. Now with her heels dug in, she stands unnoticed on the slanting round of the roof, loosening the skirts around her knees with one hand and then the other, chewing at the splinter, which is not so deep. It waggles loose. She spits it out. She bleeds a little bit.

It is her day. She has only to shimmy herself down the slant of the roof toward the low parapet, then only to stand on the parapet and fly. Only to wait until five o'clock, when the final crowd of the day will surge onto the elevator and sink toward the bowels of Paris.

She breathes.

She listens to the exclamations of the onlookers above her head—the scrape of their boots on the elevated platform, the tipsy exhilaration of their voices, the loud insistence, by a man with a contralto voice, that you can see Manayunk in the distance. "Look there," he says, and the boots above Katherine's head hurry over in one direction, and now a bird, a hawk with red in its feathers, flies near, and Katherine envies its wings.

She closes her eyes and when she opens them the eastern sky is still blue and the chestnut vendors on Broad are doing a fair business, and now Katherine smells the dying ashes of one well-behaved fire, the split skin of chestnuts. She thinks of how it will be in the air, and of how she must not rush this, must do it right, must do nothing at all at this very instant but watch the skies and the city. Lowering herself onto the roof, she braces herself against the angle with her heels, and sits with her back just shy of the window through which she has climbed.

Beneath the lid of the balcony a shadow has crept in. Above Katherine's head the onlookers have quit their hopes of Manayunk for the eastern view, where a Spanish man-of-war and its parchment-colored masts has appeared on the long arm of the Delaware, or so she hears someone say. Katherine hears the grinding maw of the Otis on its way back up—how many more elevator trips, she wonders, until the Otis is put to bed for the night? She hears the rush and scuffle of feet above her head and in the tower stairways. She has, she reminds herself, all the time in the world. She has Philadelphia and Paris at her feet, and the sky above, and now she fits her hand over her heart to quiet its patter.

Be still.

Pulling her knees up to her chin, she loosens her hair. Down on Broad she sees the boy in his blue sailor suit being tugged along by his father, out of the way from the impatient hoof of a horse that seems atrociously ill-suited to its carriage. "Pay attention," the father demands, loud enough for Katherine to hear, but the boy seems disoriented and undecided in the sunny streets of Philadelphia. He seems to have gone to Paris and stayed.

The bird, Katherine notices, is back. The hawk with its blood-colored feathers has circled near and come to rest on the parapet that rims this wide, circular roof, as if marking the spot from which Katherine herself will fly. The bird stares at her suspiciously, then cranks its head. It lifts its wings and settles them, tilts its head until she understands that it has a fascination with the window through which she has climbed. Its fascination spooks her.

"What is it?" Katherine asks the bird, and suddenly she suspects that she has been found out. It is in the bird's stance, in the curious fixing of its stare, in the sudden darkening of the shadows above her, and when Katherine turns her own head and looks up, toward the window, she understands that once again Bennett has stalked her; he has come. As if Anna had sent him out on a mission to shadow and protect her. As if her supremely selfish sister will not allow Katherine the one thing that she most wants and must have by the end of this day.

Katherine blinks, but the baker's boy is still right there in the open window, insistent.

"Don't," he says as if he can read her mind. "Don't do it."

"How dare you?" She feels her heels slipping on the angled roof and digs them in. She presses her palms into the slant to gain more traction. She turns and looks again at him.

"I saw you running across Broad," he says. "I knew."

"I'm none of your business, Bennett. I never was. If you come within another inch of me, I'll do it now," she says. "I swear I will. Leave me be."

He stays suspended—one leg through the window, his face too near. "I can't let you," he says.

But she can do anything she likes. She can still spread her wings and fly; let him explain it to somebody later; let him try, this time, to be the hero. When she is gone, what will it matter? Above her head, a baby has started to cry. Katherine digs her heels in harder and starts to stand, but the angle of the roof works against her. Instinctively she leans into the thick stone wall to catch her imperfect balance.

"Think of Anna," Bennett says. "Think of her before you do this."

"I *am* thinking of Anna," Katherine says. "All the time."

"So don't be stupid."

"Stupid?" she says.

"Stupid, yes!" His anger is shocking. This gentle boy. Her sister's lover. This baker of cranberry pies, sugar cookies, pecan tarts.

"I'm through serving Anna," Katherine says. "I won't walk in her shadow anymore. I make my own decisions, Bennett." But the more she talks, the more she feels the purpose of the day burning off her courage. She knows as well as she knows anything at all that as long as she is alive, Anna's ghost will be alive with her. A flicker and a flame. A hard knock against the heart. A voice she cannot altogether silence, nor altogether hear.

"Anna wouldn't want this," Bennett says, his one leg with its white trouser still punched through the window.

"You know nothing," Katherine answers, "about what Anna wants right now. You hardly knew what she wanted when she was alive. She let you think that you did."

But Katherine can't hurt Bennett; she knows that. She can't stop him from coming toward her, if that's what he wants. Only one window is open, and he stands within it. He reaches out his hand; she will not take it.

"Leave me alone."

"Climb off the roof."

"You've no business here."

"I've something to tell you."

"Don't you dare," she says, "start with that." But he has beat her. He has ruined everything, again. "Promise you'll leave me alone, if I leave here."

"I promise."

"Prove it to me, Bennett."

"Just trust me."

"I don't, and I won't. You're in my way."

"Not anymore," he says, retracting his long leg, leaving the window clear, all but for his hands. He reaches for her now—hauls her awkwardly up and through the window frame, which had released her to the sky. It is so much harder crawling back inside. The window is no longer wide, and she is no longer narrow. Bennett's hands on her are an abrasion.

"I'm not doing this for you," she says when her feet are through, her legs, her arms, the last trailing wisps of her too-many skirts. She shakes herself loose of him, straightens her hair, and stands by the window staring him down, daring him to say another word.

"Don't follow me, Bennett," she warns him. "Don't ever again."

Two

THE NEXT DAY PHILADELPHIA IS A STEAM SWELL, AN ASH pit, a scorcher. The next day and the next and the next, Katherine does not leave her house.

"Please," Jeannie Bea, the cook, pleads with her. "Eat."

"Love," she says. "The strawberries are sweet."

"Listen," she says. "They're bringing Master Charles's honey to the door."

But Katherine will have none of it. She paces, watching the world beyond her window. She hears the music of the fairgrounds. She remembers the beauty of Paris, the seduction of near flight, the unwanted touch of her sister's lover. His hands pulling her to safety—the very same hands, she thinks, that could not save Anna. When she falls asleep she thinks of Anna. When she wakes, her sister's ghost is near.

"It's been months." She hears her mother's voice, the shrill of it, rising up the stairs.

"Let her be," she hears her father answer. "Give it time."

Time is all that Katherine now has, too much time to remember.

Three

ANNA WAS THE MORE DELICATE TWIN. KATHERINE, ON the other hand, was sturdy, so that even though she'd been born last, twenty minutes after Anna, she'd learned early on to keep one eye out for a sister who often stood too dangerously close to things—too close to the hooves of horses, too close to the flame in Jeannie Bea's kitchen, too close to the trees during storms.

"What are you doing?"

"I'm watching."

"You can see the same thing from here."

"Not as well."

"Well enough, Anna. Please."

At night in winter Katherine would wake to find Anna at the wide-open window, leaning down toward the walk, where the moon, she said, had fallen. "Look at the moon," she'd say. "Shattered by snow."

"Mother will be angry, Anna. You'll catch your death of cold."

"She'll only know if you tell her, and you won't."

"You can't keep a cold a secret."

"Be nice, Katherine. Come and see the moon."

They were born twenty minutes apart and had the same ginger hair and green-gray eyes, though Anna's were greener. Anna's hair fell in natural curls, Katherine's in the sort of waves that had to be improved by the J. D. Oppenheimer curling tube. Still, as they got older, Katherine put herself on guard, made herself responsible for interrupting Anna's drift toward the perilous, for fixing the fences and defining the borders, the edges, the ends. Anna listened to Katherine when it was important, because Katherine's talent had never been beauty; it was saving, rescue.

"Don't go any farther than the rocks."

"But the turtles live beyond the rocks."

"I'm telling you: Don't go. You're not immortal."

Anna would say that she was a cat like Gemma, with nine entire lives to spend, all nine precious and delicious. Katherine would roll her eyes. Only once, toward the end, when Gemma went and got herself lost, did it seem that Anna finally understood that something bad could happen—that it was within the realm of possibility.

But as soon as Gemma was found again, Anna was back climbing old oaks so that she might collect a nest, snatching a pine-and-berry wreath from a neighbor's door, having to be dragged along, every day, to Girls' High and Normal School on Sergeant Street. There the lessons were Shakespeare, algebra, pedagogy, and how to draw the human figure from an odd clay model that hung like a slave from chains at the front of the room. Anna always sat in the back of the room, passing notes to Mary Phelps, polishing her shoes with the hem of her dress, and sketching Rhonda Whitleaf's nose in profile.

"Sally Biddle asks too many questions," she'd say on the way home. "She should have been a bird."

"A bird?"

"So she could squawk all day and no one would notice."

"You're horrid."

"*She* is. Why don't you notice?"

Then last April something happened; something changed. It was in the hours between noon and supper, and neither Mother nor Father were home. Jeannie Bea was in the kitchen, making terrapin stew, which Anna wouldn't eat. "It's disgusting," she said. "Eating turtles. And besides, I don't have to eat that; there's pie for dessert."

"Pie?"

"From the baker's boy, Katherine."

"What pie?"

"Cranberry pie. Delicious."

"From the bakery?"

"It would have gone on day's old. He likes me is all."

Katherine had seen the boy at the bakery on Walnut giving Anna the eye. He was tall and his hair was soft, disheveled. His teeth were white. Whenever Anna walked in with Katherine beside her, he'd give Anna the pearl of his smile. He'd give her extras of the sweet rolls they came for, and sometimes a slice of coconut pie. Anna had the world's biggest sweet tooth; that was the truth. She would have eaten dessert for breakfast, lunch, and dinner, if Mother had allowed it. What animal or bird or turtle ever suffered for the sake of a strawberry shortcake, a lemon meringue, or a cornstarch pudding, Anna reasoned. "Mother has her causes all mixed up," she'd say, but never when Mother was near, for Mother would be on her then, with a lecture.

That afternoon in April, Anna had already sent word (by way of Jeannie Bea) to Miss Louise's School of Elocution that she had fallen a bit under the weather, bribing Jeannie Bea with a pair of Jouvin real kid gloves picked up last fall at King, Seybert & Clothier.

"What did you do that for?" Katherine asked her.

"Because I had a pair already," Anna said.

"No, I meant . . ."

Spared her elocution lesson, Anna was free to go, and why in the world wouldn't Katherine consent to join her on a walk to Crowell & Granger, where the finest silks were on sale? From there they might go to the tailor at Dewees, who would fit them both, Anna was saying, for new dresses. Anna wanted one of those long jackets, to be drawn in tight at the wrists and finished with wide cuffs and a deeply flounced skirt. She thought Katherine would look best in a one-piece dress with a darted bodice. It would be their birthday in a couple of weeks, and, Anna said, they had no choice but to turn seventeen in style together. Always together.

"We have the Christmas money," Anna pleaded, and finally Katherine decided, What harm could be done? Did she really want to be her mother's child? "It's your minds that matter, girls," Mother was perpetually saying, over peas, over stew. "Knowledge prepares you for life, not fashion." Mother would prove her point by wearing the most disappointing styles. She'd leave her bonnets too wide. She'd wear the plainest cotton dresses. On the rare evenings when she accompanied their father to a function, she'd wear bustles from seasons past. The twins, especially Anna, tried not to be seen around town with their mother, but then again, Mother made that easy, with her schedule, her web of commitments to the Women's Centennial Executive Committee and the Pavilion subcommittee and the general gatherings of the Froebelists, and the special convocations to discuss the suffrage planks and the massing of like-minded females inside the Unitarian Church. "It's *your* future," Mother would say with that glare of hers, "that I am fighting for." Fighting so hard for the advancement of women that she was hardly ever at home.

One

From up high, everything seems to spill from itself. Everything is shadowed. The cool at the base of trees. The swollen lip of river. The dark beneath the cliff stones at Rockland, where Katherine had gone last week—taken the steamer, hiked to the summit, and stayed until almost too late. "Oh, Katherine," her mother had sighed the next day, her hand on the door, the velvet streamers falling crooked from her hat, her eyes fixed on the mud on Katherine's skirt. "I wish you wouldn't."

"I know what you wish."

"I'm off to Mrs. Gillespie's."

"I know that, too."

Never enough sky. Never near enough to the scooped-out wings of the hawk. Katherine walks the ridge above the river or goes all the way to George's Hill and stands two hundred and ten feet above high tide—keeping her distance from the boys and their kites, the foreigners with their funny talk and funny way of climbing. Keeping her distance to find the courage for what will be, she has decided—her last escape. Because Anna, her twin, has died, and she had no business dying. Because Anna's body, once a mirror of Katherine's own, is in a cherrywood box dug deep into the side of Laurel Hill.

Don't let me get old, Katherine can almost hear Anna saying. And look: *Congratulations, Katherine! You have granted your sister her one ill-begotten wish.*

Katherine climbs and tells no one where she is. She's climbed through February and March, through April and May, June and July. Sometimes Katherine has left the house in a light wool dress with a scarf looped loose around her neck and then, of a sudden, the weather has changed. In has blown an infiltrating wind and there Katherine has stood on Belmont Plateau, all the way up, inside the cage of the Sawyer Observatory, securing the scarf around her chin. She has stood and stared out onto the coves and hollows of the Centennial park; the great copper dome of Saints Peter and Paul; the houses, theaters, banks set tight upon the city's checkerboard squares. She has studied the unfinished pile of City Hall—like a half-baked cake, she has thought, with too much buttercream. It has never mattered how fiercely the weather has blown: Katherine has remained up high, seeking reconciliation or redemption, and finding neither.

"Anna," Katherine says aloud, "how could you?"

At home, meanwhile, Katherine's mother and father have gone on living—climbing down the stairs in the morning

"I have a gift for Bennett," Anna confided that April day.

"A gift? What gift?"

"You'll see," she said.

"Father would kill you if he knew," Katherine warned. "He's got Alan Carver in mind for your future."

"Alan Carver," Anna said, "already wears glasses."

"You can't be serious. *That's* your argument against Alan Carver?"

"That," Anna said, "and one other thing: Alan Carver isn't Bennett."

"The Carvers take care of their women," Katherine parroted her father in a false baritone.

"As if I need taking care of," Anna said, and because she laughed, Katherine did, though suddenly she felt uneasy. She sensed that something had shifted between Anna and the baker's boy. Katherine set her book of Homer aside, the pen with which she'd been making notes in a tight, blue script. She stood up to join her sister on yet another expedition. To stand guard. To make sure that nothing unforgivable happened in the pitch of an adventure.

Crowell's was but a few doors from Dewees; for once Anna's plan had some logic. Together they cut through Rittenhouse Square and headed down Walnut, where a flower vendor had set up a stall and was selling tulips, ivory-colored and, to Anna, irresistible.

"You couldn't have waited until the way back home?"

Katherine asked as Anna settled a bunch into the crook of her arm.

"I'd have risked losing them," Anna said.

It was a Saturday in April, full of sun. The harnesses on the horses in the streets looked gold instead of leather brown. The tulips in Anna's arms were already beginning to undo themselves, but Anna was oblivious.

"Did you see?" she said, for they'd crossed the broadest boulevard and were reaching 13th. "His door was open." Katherine turned and looked back. There had been a cloud of flour just outside the bakery door, the beginnings of tomorrow's bread wafting out.

"Why are we hurrying?"

"So that he won't see me."

"I thought the point was for him to see you."

"Not yet," Anna said, the color high in her cheeks. "The point is not yet. The point is to come in later, when there'll be no one but us in the store." They walked then in silence.

At Crowell's they encountered bolts upon bolts of silk; soon enough Katherine found the whole thing radically confusing. From across the room, Mrs. Childress noticed the girls and came to their aid. "What are we looking for today?" she wondered, asking first after their mother and father. Father was taking lunch at the Union League. Mother was hosting a butter sculptor on behalf of Mrs. Gillespie.

"A butter sculptor?" Mrs. Childress blinked.

"The artist," Katherine explained, "of the head of Iolanthe. You know the one, at the Pavilion? She's come all this way, from across the country." Katherine had more to say and she would have said it, but Anna interrupted.

"We're looking for something new," she said, and Mrs. Childress, turning at once from Katherine to Anna, said as if Anna had been absolute and particular, "Ah. Then. I know just the thing."

Within moments Mrs. Childress had cleared the long walnut counter and placed upon it swatches and samples so that Anna could study their choices. Anna took her time predicting just how they each would look in their proposed new colors folding into a carriage or spilling over the edge of the velvet couch in the living room. Anna knew how the dresses would appear in the glaze of the sun, and in the cameo photograph the sisters would have taken, a few weeks on, as they had for every birthday Katherine could remember. "Peridot for Katherine," Anna said. "And crimson." Looking up into Katherine's eyes, then at Mrs. Childress. "Don't you think?"

"You're agreed, dears?" Mrs. Childress asked after Katherine nodded yes, *Crimson, I guess, and peridot.*

"This one for me," Anna said, fingering the one bolt of creamiest silk, silk the color of her tulips, of a wedding.

"You're sure, then?" asked Mrs. Childress.

"I am." And then it was time to measure out the yardage, to talk about styles and trim, to sort through button boxes, spools of colored thread. In all of this, there was a leftover length of velvet ribbon—a bright red with just a hint of blue. "We'll take this, too," Anna said, and then, turning to Katherine, said, "For Bennett."

It was three thirty before the girls were done at Crowell's and then Dewees, where Samuel Black, the family tailor, had been happy to see them. The sun was laying itself down Walnut Street and the girls were walking, shading their eyes against the yellow glare. Once they reached 12th, Anna hurried faster—afraid, Katherine was left to assume, of Bennett's bakery closing for the day. She was a whole half block ahead and then an even greater distance, the tulips still there, in the crook of her arm. Finally she disappeared into the puff of fallen bakery flour, as if she were the last act in a smoke-and-mirrors magic show.

Katherine walked on, feeling too queasy to walk any faster. When she reached the door of the bakery she stopped and leaned against it, out of the glare of the sun, forcing herself to look toward the street, to betray not a hint of curiosity. If Anna wouldn't tell, Katherine wouldn't ask. She would act as if this didn't matter to her, as if Bennett were still nothing more than a passing fancy.

Only later would Anna volunteer the secret that she'd

kept from Katherine all afternoon long. "I found a nest," she said. "In the locust tree out front. Right there on one of the lowest branches. Inside was the half shell of an egg. A robin's egg. Oh, Katherine. It was gorgeous."

It was evening. They were in bed. They'd had their supper, but Anna hadn't eaten. Anna had suggested to Katherine, across the table, that the real meal waited for them, under her bed.

"You found a nest?" Katherine asked, sucking the juice of cranberry pie off of one finger. It wasn't the secret she'd expected.

"It fit inside my purse," Anna said. "I tied it with the red ribbon."

"But I was with you."

"Not the whole time."

Katherine lay in her bed, considering the wedge of moon that was beginning to push its light through their square window. She lay there in silence, weighing questions, consequences, Bennett and Anna, and Anna and Katherine, the mathematics of three against two. She considered the hard, intractable fact that Anna and Bennett would soon have words they would not have to say and a habit of turning toward one another that shouldered others away. How many times had Anna hurried east down Walnut, humming some song, holding a polished shell in her hand, a perfect pod of peas, a picture postcard acquired from the old bookseller at the farmer's market? Always something in her bag or her pockets for Bennett. "I didn't steal it, Bennett. I asked the man how much it was and he said that I could have it for free if only I could guess where the card came from. I guessed Paris, Bennett, and I was right. That woman's dress? That fall of her collar? That's how I knew." How many times? And Katherine had allowed herself to think that none of it meant very much.

She'd allowed herself to go on believing that it was still, in the end, the invincible twins. That she was equal half to an equal. Now and forever.

"He's just a boy," Anna said that night after the moon had grown brighter. "A baker's boy. Katherine?"

But Katherine made like she'd fallen asleep. She felt the ache in her teeth from too much cranberry sugar. She felt her whole heart heavy in her chest. It was true: Anna had fallen in love with Bennett; Katherine had lost her.

"What is the harm?" Anna insisted, against the silence. "Who am I hurting?"

And Katherine wanted to say, *Me, Anna! Me!* But the losses were Katherine's alone. She imagined Anna confiding in Bennett, tracing out a future. She saw now how Anna's dreams were filled with marzipan and apricot kernels, how they were pierced by a boy whose eyes were sky—changeable and cloud-swept.

That night, Katherine imagined, Anna dreamed of

Bennett—her eyes wide to the moon beyond their windows, alert to the first hint of sun. That night Katherine also dreamed of Bennett. She dreamed of Anna with Bennett. But mostly she dreamed of Anna before Bennett, when Anna was hers alone.

Four

Days have gone by. August leans into September. The sun is incessant, greedy, filling the rooms of the house on Delancey Street with the thin trails of smoke. Now Katherine stands at the window of the bedroom she and her twin once shared, watching a gull on the sill. It's as if the bird has gotten lost all these miles from the ocean, all this distance from the color blue. It is no place for a gull, not this September. But there the bird is, improbably clinging to the sill, casting a shadow on Anna's pillow. Katherine turns to see what is there. Absence, always, and condemnation. There is no escape.

And yet, Katherine thinks, this is the year of the Centennial, when all the people of the world, it seems, have come to Philadelphia. They have brought their languages, their chattering, their machines, their howling hogs and fork-tongued snakes. They have built their towers across the abominable river. *Towers,* Katherine thinks.

Katherine's mother has gone off to a meeting. Mrs. Gillespie's again, Ninth and Walnut. There are rising tensions, Mother said, among the education advocates at the

Women's Pavilion who have been drawing such a crowd at the Centennial grounds this summer. Elizabeth Peabody of Boston has raised a fuss about the handiwork of the eighteen orphans whose classroom has been put on display. "Too perfect," she has said, and this has aggravated Ruth Burritt, the teacher, who was trained for the teaching job by the country's very best. "It's growing unsightly," Mother said before she impaled her straw hat with the hard crown of her head and left. Now Katherine's father will be taking his beef and beans alone this afternoon, eating his pudding by the gas lamp in the living room.

Katherine runs her hands through the mess of her hair, and turns. She strides across the room, too big by half. She floats her hand down the banister, and her heart thumps, and her lungs hurt, and she takes one more look around—*remember this*—before she is out the door and down Delancey, cutting through Rittenhouse Square and toward Walnut Street. She reaches the southwest corner at 18th out of breath. The streetcar, she knows, will come to an eventual stop. It will take her away. It will let her finish things.

The clouds smoke across the sky and the seagulls keep their distance. A locket hangs from a ribbon of black velvet at Katherine's neck. There had been a knot of people when she first arrived at the streetcar stop, and now there are so many more. Glancing down, Katherine notices a girl, a child, with corkscrew bangs and a plaid woolen dress who is holding a bright white bird in a cage shimmered with gold.

Let the bird go, Katherine wants to say, but she doesn't.

There are women hiding from the sun beneath the silk saucers of black parasols. There are two brothers whose coats have been cut from the same pin-striped wool. An elderly man holds a top hat in his hand. The clouds are pulling away from the sun. Now the girl with the locked-up bird is singing, "Here they come!" Telling the bird, because everyone else at 18th and Walnut has already turned to see the streetcar horses dragging their cargo along. The torsos of the sorrel horses are so low to the street, their muscles so exceedingly strained, that Katherine fears the beasts will scrape their knees and topple. They pull more Philadelphians than Katherine can count—the passengers piled wide and high in the single streetcar, crammed through windows, one man clinging to the CENTENNIAL sign.

"All aboard," the cry goes out, and Katherine is swept, with the others, into the muddle that somehow absorbs the 18th-and-Walnut crowd and will quaveringly absorb the crowds all the way up to 22nd, when the horses will turn and the streetcar will heave, whining and creaking, down Chestnut, then out onto Lancaster Avenue, straight on up to the doorsteps of the Trans-Continental Hotel.

The girl with the bird holds the cage high, and the

bird beats its wings, like a fire caught behind lantern glass. Katherine's thoughts turn to Anna, two winters ago, before Bennett. Katherine had gone to market and was on her way home. She had crossed the square and had come to the white marble steps of her redbrick house, and looked up, catching a glimpse of Anna in the third-floor bedroom window, dressed only in her nightshirt, holding Gemma aloft. Even from down below, Katherine could see that her sister's cheeks were flushed. Her eyes were a green, brimming brightness. Taking her hands out of her muff to wave, Katherine called to her. "Anna!" And now Anna above her was lifting Gemma high, gesturing her twin sister in. There were only six steps, a door, two flights of steps between them, and that was too much in that moment, when they both had so much to say and no one else they wanted to say it to.

Now Gemma was moping about the house as if the cat herself had suffered the greatest loss.

The streetcar is stopped now, at 20th. Someone is a penny short of the seven-cent fare and an argument breaks out until a passenger from up above tosses a penny down and others yell, "Just get on with it. Please!" Finally they are moving again, the poor horses frothing with the heat. There is a breeze coming on. Katherine ducks an interfering elbow and glances down again at the bird, which has lifted one wing like a shoulder.

Nothing in this world is safe. Clouds form. Trees split. Horses rear. Ice breaks. Fire rages. Maybe the bird in that girl's cage is better off, but then again, Katherine thinks, the cage could crack, the prison could itself perish, along with its prisoner.

THEY ARE HEADED WEST, THE RIVER BENEATH THEM, THE hogs and the mules and the carriages all fighting for their lives, and now Katherine senses the music pulsing from the Centennial fairgrounds. She sees the colored flags blowing, smells the popcorn, the sausage, the loaves of bread. The glass face of the Main Exhibition Building flares in the sun, and everything goes on for miles.

At last the streetcar pulls to a stop at the doors of the Trans-Continental. Just down Elm, at the depot, a train is chugging to a stop. The crowd surges. Something has spooked a hackney horse; it rears, fighting with the bit in its mouth, and now the girl with the bird in the cage takes off and Katherine, too, hurries toward the patch of shade beneath the towering triangle of the Trans-Continental. It is strange here, on this side of Elm—the brick establishments plunked down between the shacks, the flimsy advertisements, the Titusville well, the famed Allen's Animal Show, promising an educated pig, a talking cow, and the rarest of sea mammals.

Katherine is caught in a swarm of hucksters with striped

shirts and canes and watches that swing from gold chains. Inside their black sack jackets and bustles and aprons they move about like hornets, and now Katherine feels a pair of eyes on her and, fearing Bennett, turns.

But it isn't Anna's baker's boy who has found her. It is a young man, his hair like wheat at the end of its season, his hands large and capable, his boots too big, a sand-colored mutt at his side. There is something familiar about him, but Katherine can't place it. She meets his stare for longer than she should, her face flushing red: *How do you know me?* Perhaps he knew Anna instead, perhaps he's a friend of Bennett's, perhaps in his mind he is seeing a ghost. She stares at him, as if she can, at this distance, unearth the truth. *Who are you?*

He is watching Katherine with bright, dark eyes. He knows her. She knows him, but vaguely. The press of the day, the crowds, her purpose, have left her disoriented.

It will all be over soon. It doesn't matter.

He isn't Bennett. That's all that counts.

There are people pushing in from all sides. There's the rising smell of beer and pie, a tainted column of smoke escaping a flue. "Out of the way, miss." Katherine hears the hackney driver when it's almost too late, when the brown horse in a lather veers near. Katherine leaps back, catching the heel of an old woman's boot.

"Madam," she says, bowing slightly. "Excuse me."

Regaining her footing, she turns in all directions, then back toward Shantytown, but the young man with the mutt is gone. What Katherine sees are shacks shouldered up against grand hotels—restaurants and beer gardens; ice-cream saloons; the museum, which is tattooed with advertisements for Borneo men and Feejees. She sees silks streaming down—yellows, pinks, the colors of the night—and flags running high into the sky. On the flat roofs of the shacks, big, messy mobs have gathered, and when Katherine looks up, she sees a pack of women dancing, lifting their skirts above the top lines of their boots, then lifting them higher as the men around them cheer. Close by, high, soars the mansard roof of the Trans-Continental Hotel, which contains, Katherine has read, five hundred rooms that can be let for five dollars a day. In the beer gardens music is playing.

In the near distance there's that girl again, the one with the bird; she's running. Across the wide avenue and down, past the Globe Hotel, leaving Elm for Belmont, where hordes of people sit sipping drinks on the open-air veranda, and couples stroll among the flower beds and horses wait for cabs to empty. All of a sudden, Katherine is on the chase, imagining, in the girl and her bird, some kind of instruction, a sign. This time she has to get it right. Soar. Swoop. Fall. She will take her instruction from a bird.

She goes down and down, through the tangle of vendors, of horses, of crowds, until finally she is out of breath and stops. She is lost in the sun-baked afternoon. There is some kind of music washing through, an overcast of sound, and Katherine folds in half and gasps for air.

When she stands straight again, her eyes settle on the sign for Operti's Tropical Garden. Signor Giuseppe Operti and his sixty-piece orchestra are set to perform this very night, Katherine learns, reading the sign, and now she decides that it's the rehearsal she hears—the tuning-up. Flutes reeling off in one direction. A violin arcing, leveling, striking a somber attitude. Drums being whisked, frenzied cymbals, the sweet duel of two oboes.

A man carrying a pleated music stand hurries by, a frail woman in an emerald skirt, a stout man with a lumpish nose, a student no older than Katherine herself, and now, coming down Belmont from the direction of the Globe, is the girl with the caged white bird. She sweeps past Katherine, innocent and untarnished by Katherine's intention to steal the bird's wisdom. She sweeps up the stairs to Operti's as if this is where she and the bird have always belonged and throws open the door, releasing a lavender scent. The girl has a square-shaped face and a minor bulb for a nose. She leans her slight weight against the door and smiles, inviting Katherine in.

Katherine follows.

Operti's is an aromatic cove of high skies and blooms. Gas lanterns float like kites overhead. Potted trees shadow the paths. There are the bright flags of celosia and astilbe, the yellow sleeves of forsythia forced well past their season, begonias the color of dandelions and fire, and in the midst of it all, the orchestra stage. On every wall, frescoes, and in the very back someone has painted a rock cliff of schist and granite, then turned some sort of spigot on, so that water, real water, cascades down. The sound of Operti's is gush and violins, the squeak of a chair, the leak of gas in a jet above, a stifled sneeze in the vicinity of the gardenias, and above that the silence of every single place that has ever lain in wait for an evening audience. By the time that Katherine has taken it all in, the girl, the mysterious mistress of the bird, has disappeared.

Katherine breathes. Miraculously, she is not asked to leave. This much beauty, she decides, is a painful thing. Paris in Philadelphia wasn't right, and Operti's isn't either.

Now from behind, from above comes a *swish-wash* of sound, and when Katherine turns, she sees the creature's wings—white as a magnolia bud in spring. The bird has been set free. It flies high, arcs wide past the suspended color globes, toward the cliff of painted rocks, the waterfalls. It swoops low and to the right, extending its wings and holding, ascending again and holding. It is the freest bird Katherine has ever seen. It leans, swoops down, and descends over the room of empty chairs and flowers and palmy heads. It drifts toward the orchestra stand where—on the very edge, between pots of calla lily and candytuft—the child sits with the empty gold cage.

She has traveled all this way, Katherine understands, to set the caged bird free. A city bird come home to a paradise, and now the girl glances Katherine's way and smiles again. Throws back her head and laughs, glad, Katherine is suddenly certain, for the audience.

"I come every day," the girl says. "My father plays the clarinet."

"The clarinet," Katherine repeats.

"My bird's name is Snow," the girl goes on.

"Imagine," Katherine answers, "having so much room to fly."

The girl tilts her head inquisitively. "I know," she says.

Above them, the bird traces out its breadth of sky. It wings over the potted palms, through the spritz of the gardenia; it fast-flutters and glides. The oboist sets aside his instrument and tilts his gaze up, and now the violinist does the same, and no one minds that Katherine has come; they assume, perhaps, that she is the child's friend.

There is a small overturned urn. Katherine arranges her skirts and plants herself there, waits for the bird to stir again. She wonders about the child and her bird, if there are others at home or if, perhaps, she is an only child.

The bird has gone off on some tune. Short, unsustained notes—more like questions than songs. The rustling of its feathers is like the sound of a hand cupped to an ear—that space between the hand and the ear, where the heartbeat echoes.

Lift.

Drag.

Thrust.

Gravity.

The mechanics, Katherine reminds herself, of flight.

Yes; she has it right: Lift. Drag. Thrust. Gravity. It will be over so soon.

On the other side of a jasmine trellis, a conversation begins. The main door opens and shuts, altering the temperature, corroding Operti's with the sounds of the outside world, with the sounds of the Centennial down the street.

"Are you going to the fair?" the girl asks, and Katherine stands, nods.

"But nothing," Katherine tells her truthfully, "will ever again be as lovely as your bird."

"We come here every day," the girl reminds her. As if urging Katherine toward a future.

Remember this, Katherine tells herself. Then she's out the door, and back on the streets, heading toward the towers of the Main Exhibition Building, where you can climb all the way to the top, take your choice of view, and lean in, hard.

Six

It is the midafternoon of Saturday, September 9, and here is Katherine now, one hundred twenty feet above the Schuylkill River, at the visitors' gate, Centennial's south entrance. She's given the keeper her twenty-five cents and he motions her inside—through the four-armed turnstile. Something clicks; Katherine's attendance has been noted. In November, when they calculate the total visitor tallies, Katherine will be counted as one of some ten million. Just a single one.

Before Katherine lies the Bartholdi Fountain, a French fantasy of sea nymphs and frogs, cherubs, turtles, and fish. The nymphs hold a cast-iron basin above their heads, as if it weighs nothing, and Katherine envies their strength then looks beyond it—to the rising and falling of the Centennial acres, the glint and silks of the buildings, the fanning women who are being pushed about in their rolling chairs, and now the Centennial rail train has come in on its narrow-gauge tracks, not far from where Katherine is standing.

"All aboard," the conductor calls, and those who wish to circumscribe the grounds by train before attempting all two hundred and fifty buildings climb in. Katherine has half a mind to join the herd, to lose herself inside the anonymous hum, but there's music coming from the Main Exhibition Building—a bold and tragic sound that floats through the building's stained-glass windows, through the spaces in between the red and black masonry, the iron and wood of the largest building in the world. The very largest one, Katherine marvels.

She rubs her hands across the silk of her skirt and turns toward the main building's west entrance. The sun has made its way to the keyhole arches. Above them are the towers and the balconies beyond the towers. A family trundles by, a troop of little girls, a man terribly taken with his new clay pipe. A shambling woman holds a package of Centennial Celery Salt to her chest, and Katherine tries to imagine her home, at her hearth, in the evening.

Over all of this the organ weeps, and now other songs have joined the song, so that by the time Katherine makes it to the west-end entrance door, the music fills the spaces in between every other thing. Katherine, exhausted, begins to make her way to the nearest empty bench. An older woman stops her. Is there something she might need?

Need?

"It's just so huge," Katherine offers, by way of a noncommittal courtesy, and the woman pats Katherine's pale hand, as if the two are neighbors or family friends, and says, "Whatever you do, save yourself for the Saint-Gobain display. You've never seen anything like it."

Katherine gives the woman a pointless smile but does nothing to extend the conversation. She finds a bench as quickly as she can and sits down. She closes her eyes against the cathedral of progress.

Seven

She remembers an evening in August, the last summer of Anna's life, shortly after Jeannie Bea had cleared the plates, when the twins' father announced his plan. "We're going," he had told them, "to the shore."

"Father?"

"Cape May," he said. "I've made arrangements. A little sea and salt will do us all good." He'd set the date for the third week in August, he said, to coincide with the Carvers' vacation. They'd take the ferry at Market Street and board the West Jersey line in Camden, to be met at the shore line by Danny, whose livery carriage would take them anywhere they wanted. Horse hooves on seashells, Katherine thought, taking to the idea at once. Promenades at high tide. The cool shelter of the beach cabin when the sun was at its harshest. Games of tenpins in the alley, and the smell of cigars in the morning, and all those Gypsy hats and flannel suits, the sound of moccasins on the hard, gray sand, corn fresh from the stalk.

"Cape May," Katherine said, while Anna repeated, "Father?" until Mother said, "It will be lovely," settling the question without the slightest enthusiasm.

"I've booked two rooms at Congress Hall," Father went on. "The *Ledger* says the oysters have been fat since mid-July."

"I despise oyster stew," Anna said. "Oysters are putrid."

"Well. It's been a good year, too, for the tomatoes."

"But the Carver family? Father?"

"It will be lovely," their mother repeated blandly, standing, flicking the crumbs from her ferociously plain dress. "Now, if you'll excuse me." She left the rest of them in their dinner chairs. She reached for her hat and turned for the hallway, saying, "Nothing is worse—you remember this, girls—than being late."

"A meeting, dear?" Father asked, without ever looking up.

"Raising stock," she said, "for the Centennial."

"Is that right?" His voice was one note, and it was hollow. It stopped their mother in her tracks.

"I wish you'd take an interest," she said.

"But you do so much," Father said. "How is a man to keep track of it all?" There was sarcasm in his voice, a sound new to the house this summer. Katherine sought Anna's eyes. Anna wouldn't look up.

"It's your century, too," Mother said. "Or haven't you noticed?"

"I notice many things," Father said.

"Precisely what things?" Mother asked.

"The noise and crush," he said, "of progress."

"Is that right?"

Katherine looked from her father to her mother. She looked at Jeannie Bea, who was keeping all expression off the wide space of her face.

"You girls go on up," Mother said after a moment. "Get some rest."

It had been raining earlier in the day, but the rain had stopped. Their mother stood in the doorway now, considering the merits of an umbrella. In the end she chose to go without. The door closed noisily behind her, like a prison door, Katherine thought. They could hear her boots on the pavement until she reached the end of their block.

"Jeannie Bea," Father said, for the room remained quiet. "I'll take my sherry on the couch." His hair was thinning, Katherine observed with shock. The lines across his forehead had ridged into something permanent, and if everyone had always said that the twins were the spitting image of their father, there were more differences between them now than likenesses. Katherine turned to see what Anna had seen, if she'd registered the same impression. But Anna's mind was somewhere else.

"Can you believe that he would do this, Katherine? Cape May? *Please*. The *Carvers*?" she moaned when the day was done.

"He's only trying to help."

"Help?"

"Well, honestly, Anna. You haven't seemed all that well."

"I'm better than well, Katherine. I'm in love. I'm happy."

"You're not yourself."

"You don't know," Anna sighed, turning over in her bed, propping her head up on one hand—Katherine could see how the shadows rose and fell, shifted themselves—"what love is."

"No," Katherine said, turning away. "I guess I don't." A spike of heat between them now. A knock against the heart.

"Alan Carver is a bore," Anna declared.

"Just think," Katherine said, not kindly, "of all the stories you'll collect for Bennett. The little secrets you will tell. The shells you'll bring home to your bakery."

"A whole *week*," Anna groaned, either ignoring the sarcasm, or not hearing it at all, which was worse, "with Alan Carver."

Silence. Katherine closed her eyes against the moon. Anna would soon be dreaming of Bennett, of his shoulders, made broad and strong by the hefting and pounding of dough. Katherine was guilty of having looked too closely, of having pondered too hard, of having imagined his attentions for herself. She was her sister's identical twin. Identical. But beauty radiated from just one of them. That was the hideous fact.

In Cape May, their mother would sit in a bathing gown and wield a pen above her pad, a scowl on her face that telegraphed concentration on matters of infinite political concern. Anna would brood and not look up from the castle she carved out of sand. Their father would sit halfway in, halfway out of the cabin, his feet dug into the hot, white sand, a preposterous hat on his head. "Looking for ships," is what he'd say. "Looking for pirates." Until finally he would announce that it was time for the daily constitutional. "Do I have takers?" he'd implore. It was a Wednesday when Katherine took the bait—as much to escape the claustrophobia of the Cape May beach cabin as to demonstrate, to Anna, what being left was all about.

They went off in silence, Katherine and her father, until their bare feet touched the advancing tide. They ambled without talking until they encountered something smaller or greater than themselves: A horseshoe crab on its back with its legs still cycling. A succession of perfect pink shells. A boy wearing a bucket on his head. A mountainous ledge of black rock in the distance. A thronging of gulls. A poked-up shovel in the sand.

Each thing was its own provocation, unearthing some memory in her father's mind, allowing Katherine fleeting access to the man beyond the banker. "The day I met your mother she was laughing," one story began, and he told that story as long as their shadows dragged behind them and even after they had gone as far as the black rocks and turned back and their shadows ran ahead. "When I was eleven,

I went to the dam to go fishing with my brother," began another, and beneath his hat his face would change into a younger version of itself. Katherine's bathing gown flapped with the breeze—its green-and-orange stripes twisting about her feet like a carousel.

The lesson, then, came in clams, an exercise in wading. "Clams work in private," he told her, leading her toward a less popular stretch of sand, an empty bucket in one hand. He turned from the water's edge into the sea, calling to Katherine to join him. He'd gone in as far as his knees, and by the time Katherine reached him the water was nearly past her waist, her loose gown swimming all around her like a swarm of green and orange fish.

"Dig with your toes," he told her, and at first she was confused, but then a wave hurled forward from the horizon and slapped high against her and just as quickly was sucked back out to sea, and in the shift of sand beneath her feet Katherine felt the razor's edge of a clam.

"Got one!" she called out to her father.

"Chip off the old block."

She pulled her sodden skirts aside and bent low to dig with her hands, the sleeves of her bathing gown turning dark and heavy at once. In the momentary calm of the sea, Katherine saw her own face reflected back at her, and in that instant it was possible to confuse herself with Anna, or to conclude that Anna had left the cabin to join Katherine and the clams. Saturated with the sea, the clam still beneath her foot, Katherine stood upright and glanced around, but it was only her father standing there, her father with the bucket of clams.

"Did you get it?" he asked her.

"Not yet," she said.

Now a new wave raised its lathered head on the horizon and began its sprint and threatened to knock Katherine off her feet. All of a sudden, she wanted to tell her father everything—about Anna, about Bennett, about coming apart. She wanted to confess the truth and be done with it, but the wave moved in with such haste that all she could do was plant her feet and hold her ground, and when it hit she felt herself fall backward, felt her father's hands on her shoulders, correcting her balance.

He was laughing, the way he never laughed, and she was laughing, too, and the gulls that had been hovering somewhat closer to the shore came nearer and screamed down, and for some reason—Katherine couldn't have said why—this made everything seem even funnier. She laughed so hard she had to gasp for air, and when she turned to see her father she saw that he was done in, too: there was a fat tear on his right cheek, making its way to his chin. When the gulls moved off, it was like a cloud blowing south. On the horizon another wave was getting ready. Katherine dug with her feet, but the clam was gone. Vanished in the shifting sands beneath her.

"I lost it," she told her father.

"There's plenty more."

So they stood, taking the waves on as a team, fixing on the clams with their feet, hoisting them up from the suctioning sand, and dropping them into the bucket, which began to strain with the weight of the thick, ridged shells. Katherine could feel the sun settling into her skin—small bursts of heat deep in her cheek and down the short slope of her nose—and she was aware of the gulls blowing back toward them, a darkening of the sea beneath those wings.

She didn't know then how much time had passed, and she can't imagine that now; she only knows, when she looks back, that the world had changed by the time they retreated with their bucket of clams. Low tide, and the wide stretch of beach was divided into the warmed, white crystals near the marsh grass, and the hard, damp sand along the sea. They left their footprints behind them, the carcass of a crab, a cluster of shells knotted with seaweed. Her father cracked the clams with a knife and tossed the pink meat to the gulls, and the gulls flew low and near behind them. The beach cabin was empty when the two returned. The castle Anna had been building had cracked—a shovel daggered right down through its middle.

"Katherine," her father said as he stood looking in on the cabin's hollow. "Is everything all right with Anna? Is there something I should know? If you tell me, Katherine, we both can help."

She looked up at him, and it hurt; she glanced away. She felt his gaze, his knowing. "I can't," is all she managed to say, turning toward him. "I can't, Pa." She bit her lip. His eyes searched hers.

"Be careful with her."

"I am. Always."

"Philadelphia's changing. The whole world is. She doesn't understand, as you understand, that there are among us dangerous neighbors."

Dangerous neighbors, Katherine thought. Wasn't Anna's baker's boy one of those?

Later it was the lodging rooms with their crisp white linens (a bed for Anna, a bed for Katherine, a dresser between them, a pitcher of iced water). It was the almost-evening bustle in the main ballroom, the games of cards, the pungency of cigars, that hour in the day when her father would sit by himself in a tall rocking chair reading a hotel copy of the paper. He'd have the sun in his face from the afternoon at the beach, and he'd seem to Katherine so much younger, as if he really had once been nothing more than a boy with a talent for mathematics.

"Your father was always smart," her mother would say, like that was the only thing that mattered, and Katherine understood that this reduced her father, for whom *smart* was its own category, incompatible with *funny*, *interesting*, *charming*. "Trust him," Katherine had pleaded that very afternoon with Anna, but Anna had refused. She would not, she said, forgive their father for the Carvers, for Cape May, for the ball they'd have to attend that night, for this horrid vacation by the sea. Anna's hair held the smell of the sea in its curls. Katherine's was collected high at the back of her head, then loosened in places by the breeze that yawned occasionally through the open window. Earlier that afternoon Anna had spread her hair across her pillow to let it dry, while Katherine had pinned hers up wet. Each in preparation for the ball that, Anna said, would be her ruin.

"I'm not going through with it," Anna announced finally. "I won't."

Her dress was the color of strawberries, her skin was cream. The twins sat knee to knee on their side-by-side beds, Katherine feeling sun-glazed and dark in her mocha-colored silk. A small distance away was the lull of the tide, the high chatter of gulls picking through the day's debris. There was the harmless creaking of a squadron of yachts that had arrived just that day from New York, the glamorous exchange of commodores. Between the cracks of the substantial door hazed the smell of a cigar from down the hall, the talk of a regatta, the anticipation of a train, promising the next wave of suitors. The waiters were already in their white ties and swallowtails, paying no attention whatsoever to the generalized hum of clerks. The evening was getting ready for itself.

"It's only a ball, Anna. It doesn't have to mean anything." Katherine kept her eyes on her hands, which seemed warped, still, by the sea. Like crepe, she thought, burying them deep inside her skirt.

"Alan stands like a vulture, haven't you seen him?" Anna complained. "His shoulders come up to his ears. He hardly knows where to put his hands; they just hang there, or else they go off on some fidget."

"But he dances, Anna. Beautifully. I've seen him. The new valse. The Merrie England. The Spanish Dance."

"Valse." Anna blew the word through her nose.

"Well, it's something, anyway. This matchmaking business is no more his fault than your own. Maybe he has his own Bennett somewhere. Some chambermaid or farmer's daughter. A forbidden love."

"He wouldn't, Katherine. I'd like him more if I thought he did."

"He comes from money."

"Why should that matter?"

"Because everything is easier with money, Anna, and you like costly things."

"Don't be absurd."

Now Katherine blew a snort through her nose, which provoked a nasty look from Anna.

"They've put me on the auction block," Anna said. "And you don't care. Or have you been too busy playing up to Father to notice?"

"Playing *up*?"

"You're already his favorite, Katherine. You always were. You could have used that to my advantage. Put a word in on my behalf. No ball. No Alan Carver."

"Anna!" Katherine leveled her sister with a glare. "I have never been his favorite, and you know it." She growled the words. "I've been responsible for you, Anna. He trusts me. That's different." Katherine felt her neck grow warm, her cheeks. She inhaled deeply, slowly deflated. She felt the seams of her mocha-colored bodice stretch, the buttons down the front put up resistance.

"We should never have come," Anna said, refusing to meet her sister's glare.

"It's not my fault that you've kept your secret a secret, Anna. If you'd have been honest . . ."

"How could I be honest? How can I be, with a mother like ours?"

"You're being unfair."

"Unfair?"

"To Father. To Bennett. To yourself. To me, worst of all. Putting me in the middle."

"I just need time."

"Is that so?"

"Don't do that, Katherine. Honest to God. Don't talk to me like that."

"I'll do what I please, Anna, actually, since you seem to do what you please, only and always."

Katherine rose from the bed and walked to the other side of the room, where more breeze had begun to blow through the window and a child's cry had got caught up with a gull's squawk, below. She looked out, then down, couldn't find the source of the commotion. When she glanced up again she saw the mist above the sea, the first small smudges of dusk above the pink horizon. She waited for Anna's rebuttal, but there was nothing, until, from that side of the room, there came the sudden shudder that one sister senses in another, a shift in things. Katherine turned.

"Why can't you stop?" Anna murmured, dragging a bent knuckle across the low path of a tear. She looked so helpless, so lost in her own beauty and in the folds of her new dress, and Katherine knew, she always knew, that she would never win against Anna. She was vulnerable, always, to the love that rose from some dark, indeterminate place within her.

You have abandoned me, Katherine wanted to answer, but the anger was entirely gone, and now she walked back across the wide-planked floor to the long, white bed, where her sister sat, face in her hands. "It will be all right, I promise," Katherine told her.

"I hate the valse," Anna sniffled. "I hate the Pop Goes the Weasel, and the polka. The galop and the reel. I hate them all. They aren't natural. Matchmaking isn't. It's the nineteenth century, after all."

"Father only wants what he thinks is best. Even if his choice is horrendous, Anna, he thinks he's looking out for you, putting you in fortune's way."

"It's a charade, Katherine, and you know it. The worst part is disappointing Father."

"I don't think the valse is so awful, Anna," Katherine said. "I'll ask him to dance."

Anna snorted behind her hands. "You'll do that? You should be sainted."

"But you have to tell Father about Bennett, Anna, and soon. Promise me that. You've turned us both into liars."

"Katherine?"

"Yes?"

"I'm sorry."

"Are you?"

"Look at me, Katherine. What do you see?"

Katherine was silent.

"Be honest. Tell me you understand." She was begging now.

"I understand," Katherine said after several long minutes ticked by. "I understand, but only partly."

"I'd protect *you,* Katherine. I'd keep every one of your secrets safe. I'd do anything for your sake."

"Is that a fact?"

"It is and you know it."

"What sort of secrets would I have, Anna? What isn't plain as day about me?" She said it beseechingly, heard the hurt in her voice. Hoped that her sister would hear it and take care.

"No heart is plain as day," Anna said instead. "Not even yours."

Later Alan Carver stood, hinged—it seemed—to the parlor wall beneath the flame of an octagonal lamp. Behind his spectacles his eyes were swollen black, and the top button of his jacket was too high, pulled tight. In one hand he cradled his pocket watch. With his free hand he kept making a fist—crunching his big bones together, then shaking them loose, like fringe. Katherine saw him first and hurried to distract her sister.

"Maybe we'll find us a commodore," Katherine said, nudging Anna to look toward the parlor's opposite wall, where the men who had come in with the sea stood at ease in their visored caps, their crisped collars.

"Us?" Anna answered, biting the haggard flesh beneath

one nail. "Every last commodore is yours, Katherine. I give them to you."

"All the better," Katherine said, "all for me."

Katherine touched the row of buttons on her dress and wished she'd packed a lighter color gown or had taken a flower from the hotel garden for her hair, something to distinguish her from the other girls who, in groups of three and four, fussed with their skirts and their hair, glanced sidelong toward the men of the sea. Mother was, she said, sitting the whole affair out; she'd had a letter from Mrs. Gillespie concerning the declaration of women's rights. Father was out on the veranda with a banker friend who was long on finishing his cigar. He had told the girls to go on; he would catch up to their good time. Anna had rolled her eyes and sighed conspicuously.

"Be good, girls," he'd said, and Katherine had said, "Pa," and Anna had squeezed Katherine's hand to make certain that she'd say nothing more, but now here was Alan Carver chewing on his tongue, and Anna, ignoring the commodores in honor of her poor, sweet baker's boy, had seen him and had let loose a little shudder. "Like a goat," she said. "There's still time before he sees us." But he'd looked up already and pipped Anna's name, and Katherine dragged her along—linked her arm into Anna's, tight—so that they might be right and proper and not embarrass, at least not yet, their father's name.

"Evening," Katherine answered for them both.

"Evening," Alan said. His eyes went from Katherine to Anna and remained there, buggy and hopeful. Anna gave him nothing—turned her gaze steadfastly toward Katherine, as if Katherine were some kind of oracle, a brand-new fascination.

"Have you had the oysters?" Alan asked, biting the back of his tongue. *A tic,* Katherine decided. *A ghastly one.* She'd not hear the end of it later that evening.

"Oysters are putrid," Anna said, not turning for an instant from her sister.

"Forgive her," Katherine told Alan. "She's being funny. Aren't you, Anna, being funny?"

"Have you had a game of croquet, then?" Alan asked. "Or a bit of tenpins, in the alley?" A small bead of sweat had formed at the part in Alan's wavy hair, and Katherine watched as it slowly worked its way down his forehead. He had freckles, Katherine noticed, pale vestiges of sun, and if you took away the glasses and the tics, the erupted rictus of his helpless nervousness, there was something kind in him, if only Anna would turn her head and notice.

"We've been at the beach," Katherine said, "collecting clams."

"Fine sport that is," Alan answered, touching his finger to his head, finding the meandering bead of sweat and interrupting its journey.

"I don't go in for clams myself," Anna said. "That's Katherine's talent." A flutter of unchaperoned girls had come down upon them, and they were laughing behind their hands, doing a poor job of keeping the various flowers in their hair. One hibiscus had turned upside down and clung to the girl's auburn hair like a third ear.

"What's that, then?" asked Alan, leaning forward to hear what Anna had said. She tipped back on her heels. Katherine stopped her with a hard clench of her arm.

"The clams are Katherine's pleasure," Anna said. "Not mine."

"And what would yours be, then?"

"Sweets. My pleasure is sweets." She nodded her head affirmatively in a way, Katherine realized, that would give Alan instant hope.

"Sherbet?" Alan asked, raising one eyebrow above the frame of his spectacles.

"Heavens no. Pies. Cranberry. I have a friend . . ."

"Oh, honestly," Katherine said, and now she looked through the crowds of the parlor hall in search of their father. He wouldn't be found. She hoped Mother would have a change of heart and salvage the moment with her arrogant competence. She put that hope aside.

"Katherine has many talents," she heard her sister say.

"Of course," Alan said politely. What else would he say? "She is your sister."

"No, actually. I'm hers. Did you know, for example, that Katherine sings?"

"Is that right, then?"

"Sweet as a bird. And at school she wins the prize for elocution. Every single year she does. She hasn't the least competition."

Katherine felt her face go warm. She saw Alan straining to give her his attention—a courtesy to Anna, who was growing more animated and beautiful the longer she went on.

"Oh," Anna said now, as if she'd only just remembered. "And Katherine dances. When Katherine dances, no one else should take the floor."

"You're growing tiresome, Anna." Katherine clamped her upper arm even harder across Anna's. Anna gave her a look, squeezed back, and continued.

"Surely you must dance, too?" Alan inquired, another bead of sweat forming at that part in his hair. The parlor had grown more crowded, and still Father had not come, and a group of girls in pastel dresses had gained their introduction to the slender commodores. Anna already had her boy at home. Katherine was tethered, doing her duty.

"Anna dances a fine quadrille," Katherine said.

"Anyone can dance the quadrille," Anna said. "Katherine excels at the new valse."

"No," Katherine said, "I don't. I've hardly practiced."

"Katherine never needs to practice," Anna insisted. "All

she needs is music, and when music plays, she dances. She ice-skates, too. Better than anyone I've ever seen. Isn't that so, my Katherine?"

Katherine leaned close to Anna and hissed, "You're embarrassing yourself."

"Embarrassing myself?" Anna said, acting shocked. "How? My sister"—she turned to Alan then, looked him squarely in the eyes, and smiled—"is terribly modest. I have to do all her bragging for her."

"Anna," Katherine said loudly now, "stop."

But Anna continued, pointing past the parlor and in through the door of the ballroom, where the musicians had begun to arrive, carrying their instruments in warped little boxes and taking small steps in their shoes. "The time is nigh," she said. "The hour approaches."

"Perhaps you'll show me your new valse," Alan said, gnawing the back of his tongue and turning, resignedly, to Katherine. The shoulders he carried up toward his ears had sunk. He'd stopped cradling that pocket watch. It had been a charade for him, too, Katherine realized. Something in him had relaxed. Anna had been right, again. And ruder than Katherine would forgive.

"It would be my pleasure, Alan," Katherine said, bowing her head and squeezing Anna's arm so hard in hers that afterward Anna showed her the bloom of the bruise on her arm—the almost midnight colors.

"It would be my pleasure," Anna said, mocking Katherine later as they lay beside each other in those beds. "My pleasure, my pleasure, my pleasure."

"You are so entirely ungracious, Anna," Katherine declared, her mocha-colored dress in a crumple on the floor, her hair spread out against the pillow, still damp with the smells of the sea. Beyond them the tide came in, and the breeze riffled the flap doors of the striped beach canopies. There was the lifted-high smell of lit cigars. There was laughter from somewhere deep in the dark of the alley. The commodores' ships, Katherine thought, were anchored in for the night, but the commodores had all gone missing.

"And you, my love," Anna said. "You're perfect."

"You'd be easy to hate," Katherine said. "If I did not love you."

Eight

After Cape May, Anna kept lying. She did absolutely nothing to reward Katherine for her faithfulness. Katherine should have seen the next thing coming, but she hadn't. She had allowed herself to believe, in Cape May, that she'd won some part of Anna back. "You're perfect," Anna had said. Didn't she mean it?

But then, on a Saturday, Katherine woke to a fever and the world swam, liquid and hot before her eyes. When she finally focused, Anna was lying propped up on one elbow, watching her.

"You've been talking in your sleep," Anna told her.

Katherine remembered nothing, not even the tail end of a dream. She tried to lift her head, but everything hurt. "My head is buried underground," she said, her words sticking to the roof of her mouth, to her tongue. A bead of sweat had detached itself from the base of one ear and begun to dribble down her neck.

"I'm going to have Jeannie Bea bring you juice," Anna told her, rising, planting her bare feet on the floor. Her hair was frizzing all around her face. Her eyes were bright. "You don't look right."

"Don't go, Anna."

"I'll be back."

"Just stay here, won't you? I can't even lift my head to drink." Katherine closed her eyes and allowed a wave of illness to wash in beneath her, then to roll over her like a tide. "I feel seasick," she said. Cape May returned. The feel of the sun on her neck. The walks beside her father along the sea. The valses—two—that she had danced with Alan while Anna stood along one crowded wall with Father, watching. Alan had led Katherine with surprising grace. He had lost all his tics within the music, and Katherine, for a moment, had imagined him a commodore, someone she had chosen for herself. "You were brilliant," Anna told Katherine later. Then: "Wait until I tell Bennett." Katherine had moaned at the thought of it. She moaned now, certain that Anna had already told, that she and Bennett had laughed together at Katherine in a way that Anna would never equate with humiliation, but that Katherine would.

"I'm getting Jeannie Bea," Anna told her.

"Nothing will help. Just stay."

"Jeannie Bea will know what to do. She always has the cure."

Katherine sank her head deeper into her goose-down pillow and conjured the full moon of Jeannie Bea's face—Jeannie Bea, who had been part of Katherine's life since forever, when Pa decided (Katherine had always been certain that it had been Pa) that the girls needed a Jeannie Bea to raise them. That they'd need someone who could warm their milk and fix their hair, who could button them into their dresses. Katherine didn't know what life would have been without Jeannie Bea, who never married for the family's sake, who took care.

Anna was slipping across the floor, going out. There was a horse in the street, three stories down. There were birds or something that sounded like birds, and then there was nothing. Katherine closed her eyes and another wave washed in. Her hair was damp, her nightgown, too.

"Child." It was Jeannie Bea now, her broad hand on Katherine's forehead. "Child, where did you get this fever?" Jeannie Bea smelled like cinnamon and fried pepper, like the darkened edges of an omelet.

"She was talking in her sleep," Anna said from within the cook's shadow.

"It's just a fever," Katherine moaned.

"A compress for your head," Jeannie Bea said. "A glass of fresh-squeezed." Producing these things, she lifted Katherine's head with her wide, chocolate-colored hand, and tipped the glass of juice toward her lips. She was slow, she was gentle as a mother. "You take the day off, love," Jeannie Bea told her. "Get some rest."

The juice felt hot in Katherine's mouth. "Thank you, Jeannie Bea," she said.

"Fever has no business here," the cook told her. "It'll be off soon enough." She tipped in another swallow of juice, then eased Katherine's head back down to the pillow. She lifted the compress from Katherine's head and smoothed the wet hair from her face. All this time, Katherine was aware of Anna standing there—a sway of color behind the solid dark of Jeannie Bea. Katherine felt the compress layered in across her brow. She closed her eyes and the wave was still beneath her.

After that, Katherine sank into near oblivion. She was aware, but only vaguely, of voices and faces, in and out. She felt her father near, in his dark suit. She heard her mother's voice in the hallway. Anna was there, then Anna was gone, then Anna didn't come back, and the waves washed in and Katherine rode them. Once she heard the squeal of a pig out in the street, the sound of someone chasing. Twice the compress on her brow was changed. Sometimes Jeannie Bea cradled Katherine's head and lifted a glass to her lips.

"Where's Anna?" Katherine remembered asking.

"She's gone off," Jeannie Bea told her. "She'll come back."

It was morning, then noon. On the third floor of Delancey Street the air was hot. Katherine's nightgown was like a crust of skin. Her hair soaked through, then dried. When Katherine opened her eyes now, she didn't feel so seasick. She felt the silence instead, the absence of Anna.

"Jeannie Bea," Katherine said when the cook arrived with toast, "where has she gone to?"

"Don't know, my child. I've had my eyes on you."

By two in the afternoon, the fever had broken. Still the room tilted when Katherine tried to stand up. "You just stay put," Jeannie Bea said when she brought Katherine a large pitcher of iced water with which she might rinse her crusted limbs.

"Anna's been gone too long."

"It's early afternoon, child. Your sister will come back."

Time wobbled. Katherine worried. She could sit up now on her own, look across the room without a wave washing in, and calculate the many hours Anna had been gone, the possibilities suggested by her absence. The implications. Had Anna been sick, Katherine would not have left her side. She knew as much for certain.

Katherine ran the sponge down her long limbs, felt the cool of the pitcher water. She slipped from the old nightgown into a new one. She sat in bed and turned the pages of *Moby-Dick*, comprehending nothing, the words a blur, the room around her only eventually losing its wobble. Finally Katherine stood at the bedroom window and waited for her sister to come home. Stood there braced against the windowsill, the heat of that summer day still rising.

Beyond the window there was a gathering of clouds at the far end of the sky, no threat of rain. One block east Sarah O'Brien was playing the piano with her window shoved open, that tedious Schubert she'd been flat-fingering all month, for her cousin's wedding. Which cousin, Katherine couldn't remember and wouldn't now, for Anna was the one who'd collected the gossip in the first place and had brought it back, and the truth was, with Anna gone, Katherine didn't feel safe. She felt a flush of heat, and then, odd and wonderful, a breeze.

There was a squabble outside, a clatter. A razzling disturbance two neighbors' yards down. Pig bedlam, Katherine realized, the same pig, it must have been, that she'd heard earlier on, and now there it was, in the blooming front garden of the Chauncers—an anarchy of spotted skin, corked tail, hoofed feet, and a young man in too-big, broken boots, with a tear up the seam of one sleeve and trousers loose at the hips, the seat of his pants good and faded. He was crouching to make himself pig-sized, cornering the hot squealing near an old bush. Thrusting the window higher and leaning out into the day, Katherine could make out the sweet talk between him and the pig, the young man doing most of the talking, promising home, that's what he was saying: "Boy, I'm taking you home. You've done and gotten yourself lost. Your master is waiting."

Katherine felt unsteady on her feet. She felt blessed by the breeze and by the young man below, who kept on standing and standing, half-crouched at the Chauncers', while the pig pawed the dirt and wagged its head and looked for an out. He was the most patient creature Katherine had ever seen—the young man in his loose trousers. He was going to wait, and he would not threaten. He would win, in the end, and take that pig home.

It was as if, Katherine decided, the young man utterly understood the pig's predicament—had put himself right in its place. As if he knew how the pig felt to be found after all the trouble the pig had done to get itself lost. "You get yourself together, now," the young man was saying. "You don't be afraid. Folks is missing you." The whole transaction going on in profile and the pig out there with the long slash of a smile, not squealing and not quite so angry, not plowing trenches into the shade of the red camellia bush.

Now the pig looked up and squinted at the sun; it seemed to take notice. So that when the boy looked up, too, Katherine saw how his eyes were like pieces of dark green-brown glass, shining and absorbing shine at the same time. She wondered if he'd seen her, then wondered why she cared, then she put her hands into the tangle of her hair and stepped back, horrified, certain that she looked a fright. When she peered out again, the young man had the pig in the cradle of his arms. He was talking to it, telling it some kind of story. The pig's hooves were kicking hard at first but soon enough they had stopped their racketeering. Now its head stopped slapping side to side until it was squatting, like a fat cat, in the young man's arms.

"Pleased to meet you," Katherine heard him tell the pig. "My name is William."

He straightened then, and left the Chauncer's yard. He closed the gate behind him. He walked down Delancey with the pig in his arms, walked west and Katherine watched him, felt sorry that he had to go. Sorry that she couldn't walk west with him. Out of the house. Out of her sickness. Out of the loneliness of not having Anna nearby.

The heat was back. Katherine closed the window against it.

It was a long time after that before Anna came home. Katherine had slept again; she had fumbled with *Moby-Dick*. She had collected herself and stood at the window. When she finally saw her sister, she was three blocks off—her body pitched forward in a hurry.

Anna was wearing a pewter-colored dress, no hat on her head. Her legs seemed loose and light beneath the layers of her skirt and she carried her elbows high so that she might keep aloft the thing she carried. Katherine had nearly sunk back into the white space of her bed by then, but in the end she'd turned at the window to face west instead of east. That's when she saw her sister traipsing down the street. Too pale and light, too fragile, too happy. Too pleased with whatever it was that she had collected in that hatbox, for that's what it was—a hatbox. Katherine opened the window to let the day in. She heard the sound of a bird singing—a reckless aria.

The sun was at Anna's back, the sky was her frame. When at last she looked up and saw Katherine standing in the third-floor window, she freed one hand and waved. "He's singing for you," she called out, and began running, her hem down near her feet. Her hands were tight about the box—that strange magenta hatbox that Anna had found one day at Dewees.

Don't run, Katherine almost called. *You'll fall.* But she was mesmerized by the sight of Anna, by the question, Where had she gone without her?

There was a penny-toss game getting under way across the street—Marty Bell and his cousins. There was a milk cart trotting by, a tabby in the gutter swatting fleas, the smell of bleach coming from a neighbor's basement. There was Jeannie Bea in the kitchen. Neither her mother nor father were home. Katherine had lost the day.

Anna was a block off, a half block, up the marble stoop. She was running up both flights of steps; she was out of breath, Katherine could hear her. When she opened their bedroom door, her face was flushed. She shut the door behind her. Laughed.

"A bobolink, Katherine," she said. "Hurry. Close the

window." Speaking as if Katherine hadn't just been roused from a fever, as if she hadn't only but recently summoned the strength to stand at all. "Oh, honestly," Anna said when she saw Katherine not moving, watching her. "Darling." She slipped the box onto her bed, then crossed the room and shut the window. "You're looking well," she declared, staring deep into Katherine's eyes.

"I've been sick all day. Where were you?"

"Jeannie Bea knows all the cures. I only know how to amuse you."

"*Amuse* me?" Katherine repeated. "Where did you go?"

"I've been trying to tell you. Stop asking questions, and I will."

Anna crossed the room again and collected the box from her bed. She held it firmly with both hands, but gently, too. "A bobolink," she said. "For you." And now like an illusionist with a practiced trick, she freed the box of its slightly askew lid—such a strangely hued box, Katherine thought, so like Anna to be out there toting a bigheaded color. Into her free hand, Anna scooped up the bobolink and let the bird stretch one wing and settle, let the bird flaunt the bright coal-blackness of its feathers, the drifts of snow-white across its small, proud back, the straw-colored drift down its back. The bird cranked its head right, and blinked.

"Come on, bird," Anna encouraged. "Show Katherine what you're made of." Katherine could see the pulsing heart in the bird's elastic chest, the cinders of fear in its eyes. Quietly, sweetly, Anna began to hum until the bird gave up its song, which wasn't shrill and wasn't haunting, just a daylight summer song.

"He's a soprano," Anna said.

Katherine closed her eyes and took a long, dry breath. She thought of Cape May, just a week before, and the promises she'd thought the sisters had made to each other. "Where did you get him?"

"By the river. The Schuylkill. Oh, Katherine. It was such a day!" Anna moved toward Katherine and brought the singing bird closer. It spread and settled its wings but made no move to fly.

"By yourself?" Katherine leaned away from Anna and against the window harder.

"No," Anna said, her words growing sharper. "Not actually. Bennett was with me."

"Isn't that nice?"

"Yes. In fact it was."

The bobolink was growing restless in Anna's hands. She turned from Katherine, slipped across the room, and lowered the bird into the box. She slid on the lid, leaving enough room for air, then turned back around to Katherine, hands on her hips. There were dull green stains on one elbow of Anna's dress. The choker she often wore was missing.

"I thought Bennett was working," Katherine said flatly.

"I went to the bakery to find you something sweet. I thought that maybe it would help, maybe it would make you feel better. But Bennett said that maybe you'd like wildflowers instead, that the shop was slow, that he could come with me. I came home. I got the hatbox. You were sleeping. He met me in the park."

"You came in and out and I didn't hear you?" Astonished, Katherine searched her memory, but the morning was oceanic, elastic, a blur. The morning had been Jeannie Bea, and her mother's voice in the hall, her father's dark suit, a cool compress on her head. The morning hadn't been Anna.

"You were talking to yourself in your sleep. Katherine. Darling. You had a fever."

"Wildflowers," Katherine said unhappily. "In a hatbox." She turned and stared out the window, where outside Marty and his cousins were gathered on his stoop, their game of penny toss over.

"It was the biggest box I had."

"Weren't you afraid someone might see you?"

"See me?"

"Out and about with your baker's boy?"

"I'm never afraid, Katherine, except when you want me to be." Anna laughed but Katherine didn't. She walked to her own bed, sat down on the stale sheets, didn't trust her spine to hold her. "If only you'd come," Anna said appeasingly. "There was a kite, an orange one, above the river. And there were turtles, Katherine. A herd of them. We went all the way to the boathouses, hunting for your flowers."

"Isn't that nice?" Katherine said again, dully.

"They're painted so pretty."

"The flowers?"

"No," Anna said. "The boathouses. And the scullers and coxswains and crews were out, and the shade beneath the pines was blue. Blue, Katherine. I was wishing you could have seen it. I swear that I was."

She sounded defensive and small, but Katherine wasn't in the mood to forgive her. Anna had never told the truth to Pa. She had not stayed home when Katherine, her protector, her secret keeper, was ill.

"Don't say what you don't mean."

"We went to get you *flowers*." Anna's cheeks were flushed now, her eyes sharply accusing. "But Bennett found the bird. The bird was better."

"*Bennett* found it."

"It seemed lost."

"I see."

"It fit nicely in the hatbox."

"Yes?"

"You're being horrid, Katherine. I brought you a gift."

"Hardly," Katherine said. "Seems I gave you one."

"Listen to you." Anna turned, collected the hatbox, stood.

"Where are you going?"

"I'm not amusing you. That's clear. It's rather tedious, actually, to be here with you."

"You just arrived."

"And now I'm going."

"Anna?" It was Pa, calling up from the bottom of the stairs.

"Yes, Pa?"

"Katherine okay?"

"She's resting, Pa." Anna shot Katherine a look. "I was just going out to get some air."

She threw a little curtsy. She spun on her heels. She was gone. It wasn't until so much later that night that Anna came to bed—she slipped into their room, threw open the window, stood by the moon. It was as if she was waiting for Katherine to talk, giving them both a second chance. But Katherine wouldn't turn. She wouldn't look her sister in the eyes. A while later, Anna was gone—across the floor, out the door, and down the wide-planked steps. Into the darkness with Bennett.

"What a *stupid* thing to do," Katherine accused Anna, the next morning, near dawn. She'd been lying there in their room through the whole night alone, her fever gone, her mind restless. She'd been willing herself to stay where she was, to not go running after her sister again; to let Anna take the consequences, let Anna be damned. Katherine had lain in bed, her heart loud and ugly in her chest, her thoughts teetering between revenge and regret, and for the longest while there were only the acrobatics of a squirrel up on the roof, and then the early morning finch set in. The skies were scored with lemon and pink before the latch slid back on the wide front door, and the footfalls rose, and Anna arrived, breathless, her boots in her hands.

"Don't call me stupid."

"You are. Look at you. Like a cat in the night."

"For God's sake, Katherine," Anna said. "Be civilized." Anna raised her hand to her ruined hair and primped it ineffectually. She ran her fingers down the buttons of her thin overcoat, fondly, absentmindedly, the trace of a smile still caught on her face, not a single ounce of remorse.

"And are *you* civilized? Sneaking out to a river by day, to a park at night, to wherever you've just come from—with a baker's boy, Anna? *Alone?* You could be dead. Who'd know where to find you?" Katherine heard her voice rising, and she didn't care. She knew she was in danger of blaring her sister's affair to the world, and frankly, why shouldn't she? Anna was treating Katherine as if she were their elder. Treating her as if she couldn't be trusted. Which was the same thing, absolutely.

"You'll wake Mother, Katherine. Please." Anna walked

to her side of the room and sat down. Perched on the edge of her bed with a straight back, that infuriating smile still on her face, as if no argument could dislodge her from her pervasive happiness.

"And I'm supposed to care? I'll wake the whole of Delancey, if I wish. You're ridiculous. Everything you're doing is selfish." Katherine wouldn't turn in her bed. She lay stiff, furious.

"You ought to give him a chance before you start accusing. Get to know him. Stop being such a snob."

"I'm not talking about Bennett. I'm talking about you."

"This is about you, and you know it. You were always jealous. Always so grim, Katherine. Never acting your age, and boys see that. Bennett does."

"So you've been speaking of me, then. To him." Katherine felt flattened, the betrayal final.

"Not a lot. Just some."

"You're worse than I thought, Anna. You'll stop at nothing."

"Where's your heart?"

Katherine didn't answer, didn't know how. Soon the silence was worse than any accusation, and now Katherine turned and saw how Anna was slipping her boots back on, buttoning each button with a frightening calm.

"What are you doing?" she demanded.

"I'm going out."

"You just came in."

"I won't waste the day fighting with you."

"Anna." Katherine pushed off the bed now. She stood, her bare feet on the rose-colored rug. "Don't. Please don't. I'm sorry."

But Anna had made up her mind. She was across the room and out the door and there was the sound of her boots going down, words with Jeannie Bea, the unlatching and latching of the front door, and now the pattering away on the walk. All that summer morning Katherine remained in their room, looking out as the day became itself, thinking Anna might return. When Jeannie Bea called for breakfast, Katherine excused herself. When Pa knocked on the door, she said she was lying in bed with a book.

"What happened, love?" he said. He stood above her, blocking the rise of the morning sun. She couldn't meet his eyes. She turned.

"Anna was bored."

"She seemed agitated, not bored. There's a difference, honey." As if her father could bring his math to this, his economics and his rule book.

"Why don't you ask Anna, Pa? Please. Leave me out of it for once, will you? It's Anna's turn to speak."

"Your sister's elusive."

"My sister isn't me."

"But whatever she's doing is affecting you. I asked you what happened. I'm asking after *you*."

She looked up and she saw all the care in his face, the solemnity of responsibility, a trait they shared. She felt tears welling within her. She turned again, her father's shadow still saving her from the sun.

"I can't talk right now, Pa."

"All right, then," he sighed.

"I think I'd like to stay in bed awhile."

"Moby-Dick," he said.

"I'm trying."

"It's a good book," he said, "once you get in thick with it." He touched Katherine's forehead with one finger and stayed hovering above her for a long time. Finally she turned and looked him squarely in the eyes.

"Thank you, Pa," she said, and he leaned down and kissed her where his finger had been.

Later there was sun, too much sun, everywhere. There was an entire blast of morning heat in a room hollowed out but for one.

Nine

THE SUN SPILLING IN THROUGH THE STAINED-GLASS windows daubs hatbands and dresses with diluted colors—red gone slightly copper, blue like the final hour of a bruise, green like the eyes of a cat. From the nozzles of the Venus fountain, water geysers toward the ceiling struts then collapses into iron basins and pools, and now Katherine, opening her eyes with a start, feels a trickle of heat run down her cheek, past her ear.

She plays the scenes of her sickness back across her mind's eye, this time more slowly. She stands at that window in that bedroom on Delancey Street, looking down and waiting for Anna, and studying, as she does, that boy with the oversize boots and the pig, that boy with the gentle hands and the way of speaking, and now at last she knows precisely who he is. The boy with the pig is the boy with the mutt who was there, this very morning, near the streetcar. The boy in the chattering chaos of the Centennial, who had seemed to know who she was. Who had watched her and dared her to speak, to say hello.

It was the same boy—not just from that day with the

pig, but from another, in November—a brisk, unnerving day that had started out all wrong and had only grown worse, and had borne, within itself, more seeds of the coming disaster.

The seeds, in fact, of today. Katherine allows herself to remember because she won't ever again. Maybe the Centennial Exhibition is the story of the future. Today is the story of Katherine's past, which was also Anna's.

That day, last November, had begun with breakfast. It had begun with Anna sitting directly across from Katherine, a million miles away. Anna had been running her spoon over the side of her egg like the egg was a clay sculpture she was smoothing. She'd been sitting there, saving her best thoughts for Bennett, leaving Katherine out in the cold. Time apart from her baker's boy was a torture for Anna. Still, on that day Katherine desperately wanted to be with her sister. She'd overlook her sullenness. She just wanted company.

So they'd gone out, that Saturday, shopping. They had a list of things that were to be bought, and Katherine, tentative, linked her arm with Anna's, and Anna let her, dutifully, though they both, Katherine realized, remembered the bruise of Cape May. "We'll get some ice cream," Katherine said, but then Anna, of course, had a better idea.

"No. We'll get shortbread for free at Bennett's."

"I'd rather have ice cream."

"We can have that, too."

"Do we have to go to Bennett's?"

"Yes. We do."

They did their chores. They went out and about, buying buttons for Jeannie Bea and a new kind of tea for their mother and tobacco for their father, and then they stopped at a corner shop to look at ready-made coats, to each try one on for the winter. They left Wanamaker's with two pairs of muffs instead. Anna's was white and Katherine's silver. And then they were on Walnut Street and past Broad, and the puff of bakery flour was floating aimlessly overhead, like the last blow of a train stack. They were there, at the baker's, where Anna said, "Please, dear. Watch the door." And so Katherine stood as Anna told her to stand—her face toward Walnut Street, her back to the bakery, her near happiness of just a few moments before threading itself into a black hole.

"Tell whomever asks that the shop is closed," Anna had instructed Katherine, sliding in through the door, and Katherine had glared at her, and yet she stayed, a sentinel on that mild November day. The skin against her brow and cheeks felt taut. Her new muff hung from her neck; her hands were nervous. She shuffled back and forth in polished boots, waiting for Anna to finish.

And then, from down the street came the young man with wheat-colored hair, his trouser pockets bulging as if stuffed with eggs, his arms filled with a hen so still that Katherine at first concluded that it was someone's unplucked dinner. The closer he came, the better Katherine heard the click of eggshell against eggshell, an odd, sweet sound. The nearer he came, the better she saw how the hen in his arms blinked, perfectly calm, perfectly still. Now he was a few feet off and slowing his pace. He dared to stop, to ask Katherine a question.

"Cream biscuits today?" he asked, thrusting his chin in the direction of the shop and waiting for the answer, casual, as if a hen were not sitting squat in his arms, twisting its neck, proudly displaying its comb. As if a breeze had not just now blown in, ruffling the old hen's feathers.

He had no business speaking with her.

He knew it. So did she.

He was from another side of town. He was from another place. *Dangerous neighbors,* her father had said.

"Baker's stepped out," Katherine informed him. "Come back tomorrow."

His eyes were the color of a river at night. He smelled like straw or hay, like the tang of a goat's warm hide, like the eggs warming in his pocket. Katherine studied him, decided against deciding he was handsome, though he was—undeniably he was. This close up he was even more handsome than he'd seemed from her bedroom window, for this was when it struck her: he was the boy with the pig. *My name is William.* She ignored him, best as she could. She stared back out toward the street. Anyone passing might have thought she'd known him—that a poor boy and a banker's daughter had gotten themselves into a tangle. Not possible. She felt him studying her face, the fade of freckles across the bridge of her nose, the space between her two front teeth. Her unwillingness to be charmed or to be charming. The lie she was so obviously keeping.

"Warm for November," he said, almost a game now, to see if he could force a conversation, get her to say something, at least, about the wisdom of a muff in warm weather.

"It is."

"Birds don't know what to do"—he stopped, looked for a reaction—"in weather like this." The hen sat up straighter. Katherine blinked, gave nothing away, didn't want him to guess that she'd seen this boy once, months ago—felt, indeed, that she already knew him.

Now she watched William glancing back into the shop, toward the gleaming display case and the three glass-domed cake trays, the bowl of glacé cherries, the polished register, the pair of metal tongs. She saw him press his face harder against the door so that he might see even deeper into the shop, and now, afraid for what he might see, for how he might expose the sisters and their subterfuge, Katherine tried to distract him.

"The hen," she asked, "is it yours?"

"It was lost," he said. "I went and found it."

"So that's your game?"

"My game?"

"What you do?"

"I rescue lost things. Horses, cows, pigs, dogs. Dogs, mostly. Doesn't pay too bad, either. You should try it."

He laughed but she didn't. The hen didn't stir and William wouldn't turn. He just stood there, beside Katherine, so close that she could touch him, so close that she saw every inch of what he saw, beyond the bakery door. She leaned forward, despite herself. Felt his sweet breath upon her ear—warm, she thought; she should not have thought it. She took it in, like he did—the row of buttons in the far corner of the shop and how they flared with the sun. The whispering of voices; the rustling of skirts against hands and knees; the single word, "Anna." Katherine could see her own sister dressed unseasonably in cream, her hair a wilderness, the baker's fingers low on her neck, the buttons across her chest loose and handled. Bennett was a good head and a half taller than Anna. He had to lean down to take her in, and so she was on her toes, her face spooned up toward him, oblivious to all things but his kisses.

Katherine felt William at her side turn and assess her differently. She felt her face go hot, her eyes go hard as marbles, her whole self deflecting his questions. *Don't ask me.*

"Come back tomorrow," Katherine finally said. "Bakery is closed for the moment."

"As you please." He stepped back out onto the walk,

took a gentleman's bow. He said nothing, and he could have; she was defenseless. He doffed his hat and took the hen and the hen's eggs back to whomever had lost them, and what she felt then, what she registered for later—for now, for right this minute at the Centennial, her last day ever, an hour before her flight—was that he did not walk away in triumph, pleased for her shame, pleased with his knowing. He walked away so that the hen would stay still, so that the eggs in his pocket would not crack. She heard the sound of those eggs in his pocket, moving west, down Walnut Street. She remembered that other afternoon, months before, when the pig was rescued from the Chauncers'—how he had trailed off and left her lonely.

Wait, Katherine almost cried after him, but he was quick on his feet, and she was alone again, a sentry, condemned to listening to the sounds of Bennett and Anna, within. To the conversation that had, somehow, kicked up furiously between them.

"I don't know where she is, how she got out," Anna was saying. "Katherine will blame me. She'll say it's all my fault."

"You'll find her," Bennett reassured.

"But I've looked already, and Gemma is lost. And she's such a sweet cat, Bennett."

"Cats come home."

"I won't be forgiven. Oh, Bennett. You can't possibly

know what it's like to have a sister whom you're forever disappointing."

Forever disappointing. It was, Katherine thought that day, the end. It was irreparable—Anna saying such a thing to the baker's boy. That day, Katherine went home and did not wait for her sister. She marched upstairs and slammed the door. When Jeannie Bea called up after her, asking for Anna, Katherine said, "I've no idea where she is, and I don't care."

She thought she'd be able to live with that. From now on. To not know and to not care.

For weeks it went on like that. For weeks, Katherine pretended that she had no more interest in her twin—their roads had diverged; their futures were separate. At school, Katherine consorted with Libby D. She stayed afterward, or walked home separately. She wouldn't wait for Anna when she called.

"What's *wrong* with you?" Anna would ask her at night.

"What's wrong with *me*?" Katherine would say. And that was all.

But then, there was New Year's Eve, just weeks before Anna disappeared altogether. Katherine was more lonely than one person can survive. That night, when Anna sighed, "Oh, I'd love to see the fireworks," and Katherine realized that the baker's boy wasn't a likely escort, Katherine said, "I'd like that, too," and they bundled into their coats, and went out.

Katherine and Anna cut through Rittenhouse Square, where the society people had gathered in their wools and silks, hats on the men's heads, muffs hiding the porcelain hands of women who left their work to others. The banners strung from the upper stories of Walnut Street snapped whenever a wind blew through. The twins had gone out wearing matching gray coats and blueberry silks. In the gaslight, Anna's hair shone bright as the flesh of a ripe peach, then faded to a glimmer in the shadows. A mist was either falling or rising; in the amber of the gaslight it wasn't possible to tell. The air seemed bothered.

Already the revelers were out. Masked mummers with banjos thrown across their backs, feathers trailing. Gangs of toughs. Children who ran, squealing, one after the other, in the direction of Independence Hall, their parents and neighbors on the streets behind them, beneath the banners and the flickering lamplight, behind a young man who carried a goat in his arms, a sandy-colored mutt following at his heels. The crowd was thickening. The children taunted one another with the promise of dynamite, with the sight of Mayor Stokley, getting ready to raise the flag. Like everybody else, Anna and Katherine went east—their wraps blown open by the wind, the mist at their feet, Anna scanning the crowd for Bennett, Katherine trying to pretend she didn't see.

From Ninth all the way to Sixth and north to Chestnut, they went, Katherine trying to tease back Anna's attention, Anna sometimes unlocking her arm from her sister's, darting ahead, before Katherine could reach her again. Finally, at Independence Hall, they were stopped with the crowd, and Anna had nowhere to be but beside her sister. One mummer had raised his banjo over his head and was finger-strutting on the strings. An old hag was keeping time with the blunt end of her cane. A boy was daring another with a stick tipped with fire, and the goat in that young man's arms stayed still. Anna was tied, too, but looking out over the crowd, ready to bolt at any instant.

Now Mayor Stokley was hitching the flag up the pole. Now the flutes began to play, the drums and banjos, clarinets, piccolos, cymbals—not a song, but bass against fiddle against the cries of the crowd, against the hiss of the fire on the one boy's stick, a wild din. Then the mayor was making an announcement, and the crowd, all in one voice, cheered, and then, piercing and unmistakable, came the steel whine of the first firework—a white wail through the misted night that burst wide open into suspended sparks of color. *Like a spider's web*, Katherine thought, watching the color scatter across the sky. Another cannon went off. The sky was scrambled. Katherine stared skyward and for one forgetful moment thought only of herself and the sky.

She felt a loosening, a lightening. Her arm went slack,

and she recognized, too late, that Anna had fled. She was tunneling through the crowd, running across Fifth and down Chestnut: running. East, under a sky that was aluminum and glittered copper, through a noise Katherine could never describe. East, to the very edge of the city.

Anna's blueberry skirt was kicking up above her boots. Her gray wrap was flying out behind her. Where, Katherine wondered, was she going, and why would she not stop for Katherine? Why would she force Katherine to take off running, too, past the banks, past the market, past the rows of brick homes and marble lintels, over cobblestones and streetcar tracks, past a ravaged horse tied to a thick lamppost? Anna ran. Katherine had to run faster. *Bennett,* Katherine thought, but it wasn't him. Tonight, in fact, it wasn't.

And it wasn't until Anna had gone all the way to the city's edge that Katherine stopped running. Not until then did she understand that the river was here. The wide, black Delaware that hemmed Philadelphia in on its eastern side and that held now, on its slickened face, the mirror image of the sky. Whatever broke open up above was breaking on the river, too, and if you were out on the Delaware, if you made your way past the docks and lowered yourself down and stood or floated, you'd be inside a globe of fizzing color. Anna stood near the edge; Katherine came closer. She reached for Anna as the colors broke over the sky, over the river. But still Anna shrugged her sister off and walked out even closer to the edge. She was breathing hard. By now they both were.

"Don't you dare, Anna," Katherine said. "This is as far as we go."

"It's just a river, Katherine. It's harmless."

"No, it's not, and you know it."

"It's the New Year."

"I know what it is."

"I just want to get closer."

"Anna," Katherine warned, and Anna threw her bright head back and laughed, then all of a sudden grew somber.

"I couldn't find Bennett," she said. "All of Philadelphia in the streets, but Bennett wasn't there."

"He was probably out somewhere, searching for you," Katherine said grudgingly.

"Oh, Katherine," Anna sighed. "Do you think so?" She turned at last to look at Katherine, to study her with eyes that were, if full of fierceness, sweet. Then she opened her arm to Katherine, and the sisters stood as the river held its mirror to the dazzling New Year's sky.

Anna leaned in close. "I forgive you," she said.

"For what?"

"For caring so much that it makes you mean."

"He'll ruin us both," Katherine said, but not out of anger this time.

"Look in his eyes sometime. Try and see him."

"I have, Anna. I understand. I know why you love him."

"I'll marry him."

"But Father won't allow it."

"Perhaps Mother will, then. Pursuit of happiness. Constitutional and whatnot."

"You're slightly mad," Katherine said.

"Of course I am." Anna laughed. And then she turned toward Katherine and leaned in for a kiss. "Love you," she said, and Katherine thought, *Remember this.*

That night Katherine gave up trying to talk sense into Anna. That night she did not try to argue her twin sister out of her gargantuan joy; she did not try to save her. It was then that Katherine decided to begin to look the other way on purpose, but this time without anger, without the intent to prove a point. She decided to stop protecting Anna, so that she might love her more truly.

It was a decision she had made. She didn't foresee the consequences.

Ten

Now at the Centennial, a barbershop quartet prepares to sing, and whoever has been playing the organ has disappeared. *More smoke,* Katherine thinks. *More mirrors.* The afternoon is running on and Katherine knows that if she's serious about letting it all go, she must begin to move toward her final destination.

She zags in and out of inventions, finds herself at the telegraph just as a message gets tapped to another corner of the globe. The crowd masses and moves, and Katherine moves with it, like a leaf floating on the back of a wet current.

The wonders of the world slide past. Parisian corsets cavorting on their pedestals. Vases on lacquered shelves. Folding beds. Walls of cutlery. The sweetest assortment of sugar-colored pills, all set to sail on a yacht. Brazil, she discovers, lives inside its own Frank Furness–designed house with its own flowers made of feathers, its own yams and sarsaparilla.

"Excuse me." It's an old man with a barking brogue—a man with a cane—and Katherine's in his way. She's not even sure how she got here, what secret internal engine brought her down one aisle and up another and through vale and hill and plains toward here, between the countries of Holland and Belgium at the entrance to the Moorish palace of Brazil, with its decorative arches and wooden pillars. Everything above is color—yellow, red, green, blue panels of painted wood—and wedged into the color are iridescent tiles that spell the names of provinces.

More insistently this time, the man pounds the floor with the end of his cane. He clears his throat. "Please," he says.

"Forgive me." She steps aside, into the kingdom of Brazil, where before her now is a bouquet of blooming feathers. Beyond the bouquet is a case of butterflies pinned into false flight and next are insects that will never lose their gleam. Brazil is here in photographs, in maps, in charts, in the native ingenuity of manioc, castor tree, mahogany, laces, and wool hats, in the strong odor of leather saddles and tribal hammocks.

She weaves back and forth across acres. Past zinc ore and printing inks; a library of blank books; a cabinet of violins; an iron letter box; a woman in a rolling chair, a pink-nosed pup upon her lap. The man selling Centennial guidebooks smiles, inviting a sale. Katherine shakes her head no, for how could a book explain the stuffed Russian bear hanging from his toes, the jars of black powder, the wall of soda ash?

At the intersection of the main aisle and the central

transept is a palace of jewels: Tiffany, Starr & Marcus, Caldwell. If you see nothing else at the Centennial, see the jewels, Katherine had been told. See these cinnamon-colored cameos; this diamond necklace; these perfect solitaires; these black, white, and pink pearls. She waits her turn before sapphire and ruby, before tiaras, before the famous peacock feather with the massive Brunswick diamond nestled within. *Precious.* It's the only word that comes to mind, and suddenly she feels terrified of all that will begin today, and of all that will end.

Behind her, in the open aisle, something is wrong. Katherine senses a low-grade panic, and in an instant, turning, she understands: a child is missing and a mother is blaming herself. "Darcy?" the mother has begun to call. "Honey?" An elderly woman beside the mother says, "Tell us what she looks like, dear. She can't have gone far."

"But she was right here," the mother insists. "There." She points to a place by her feet. She turns and takes a few steps west, a few east; she circles back, clearly afraid to go too far, to leave the daughter's starting spot, and now a small surge of strangers has gathered, now more questions are being asked, now the mother grows increasingly confused. Katherine hears herself repeat the question, "But what does she look like? Your daughter. How old is she? How big?" She repeats herself, until the mother understands that she is only trying to help.

"Four years old," the mother says. The hair has fallen out from beneath her hat; her eyes are desperate and black. "In a pink dress. Darcy's sherbet dress, she calls it. She was right here. I was here. And she was there, beside me." The mother gestures toward her own shadow again; she raises her arms, bites the bottom of her lip.

"We'll find her," Katherine says, wondering where in the world her sudden confidence comes from. "You stay where you are." Just like that, as if she knows where a girl might go in a place like this, she takes off in one direction, hearing the mother's cry at her back: "Darcy? Honey?" Katherine runs, remembering Anna, remembering that day in winter, when she could not move fast enough, when she could not, did not, save her sister.

When she let it happen.

Past the Leviathan Ostrich Incubator, past the pyramids, past the tower of wine bottles, past buttons and straw hats and tie silks, past the fire clay and slate, the bandstand, another iron letter box, the faces, and in all that distance, no little girl in sherbet pink. A quarter hour goes by at least, until at last Katherine turns a corner and sees a child alone, at the display of Watson nutshells. A child, tantalized and unafraid. The girl is amazed, Katherine can see, by the dangling oddities, the carved nuts and fruit stones that hang as if from the rims of a giant birdcage; Katherine is amazed that she has found her, that rescue remains a possibility. Too short to reach the nearest ornament, the girl is stretching nonetheless, balancing on her toes, not nearly lost in her own mind, not nearly on the verge of being found.

"Darcy?" Katherine says quietly, so that the girl won't run. "Are you Darcy?" The girl falls off her balance and takes in the spectacle of Katherine, whose face is flushed, whose heart is high and wild, whose thoughts are seized, again and again, by images of Anna, a memory, now, of Mother, once she came to understand the irreversibility of Anna's being lost. "Your mother has been looking for you, Darcy," Katherine says. "I can show you where she is."

"Did you see the nutshells?" Darcy asks.

"I did," Katherine says, taking the girl's hand.

"Do you think they're pretty?"

"Very pretty," Katherine says.

The little girl nods.

"This must be your sherbet dress."

"It's pink," Darcy says.

"It's a nice pink."

The girl's hand in Katherine's hand is small and complete. An anchor in a vast sea.

Katherine stands and listens to the bedlam noise of the Exhibition Hall. She closes her eyes, for maybe that will help her hear the voice of Darcy's mother, calling. If not the word, *Darcy*, won't Katherine hear the thrash-sound of fear, for she knows how that sounds, what it sounded like that day, when she called out Anna's name, and Anna did not answer, and Anna would not answer ever again.

"Let's find your mother," Katherine says, and Darcy is content to go on with this ginger-haired stranger, though she glances twice over her shoulder at the glamorous display of nutshells as now the two trace backward, toward the Brunswick diamond. There is the iron letter box—is it the same one? There are the straw hats and the tie silks, and they, at least, are the same, and now beside the towering wine bottles is Darcy's mother, who is bent forward at the waist, as if every fiber of herself has already been damaged by the possibility of loss.

"The nutshells," Katherine says, and Darcy's mother turns and looks up at Katherine, then down at Darcy, and her eyes do not know what to do.

"You found her," she says, barely a whisper.

The mother hurries forward and lifts Darcy up into her arms and locks her in close, as if she will never again let her go.

"I don't know how to thank you," she says to Katherine, over Darcy's squirming head, the little kick of her legs. "I don't know what—"

"Please," Katherine says, putting up her hand, stopping the mother from coming any closer. "It was nothing." And it is nothing; it does nothing to bring Anna back. It had been

Katherine's job to keep her sister safe. It had been Bennett's obligation. Both of them failed, and now Katherine recalls the look on Bennett's face that fatal day, and suddenly she is certain: he is there somewhere, among the crowds; he has followed her; he is waiting. This afternoon in the Main Exhibition Hall of the Centennial, she feels sick with knowing that he will attempt to stop her again. That he cannot, just as she cannot, let this business go.

"Excuse me," she says to Darcy's mother, who reaches out toward Katherine, but she is gone. She is escaping into the crowd that has massed around Tufts—all those people waiting for a soda pop. She can camouflage herself here, she thinks, until she carves out her plan.

And so she moves through the crowd and toward the fountain statuary, toward the only open squeeze of space at the narrow bar. Sliding into place, she says to the girl across the counter, "An orange soda, please."

The girl is as pallid as her uniform and in no hurry to please. She adds Katherine's order to her list of orders, tells Katherine it could be some time, saying, "We're busy," as if Katherine herself hasn't looked about. Katherine can only wait. She checks over her shoulder. Nobody could find her here.

"Makes you wish you were in the soda business, don't it, though?" says the man to Katherine's right, a rasping voice, but not an old one. Turning, she notices how it is that he's either lost his jacket or left it behind, and how to his vest he's pinned a dozen gold watches, like buttons sewn into the wrong spots. He watches her watching. She feels his eyes on her and blushes, and her embarrassment pleases him so much that he smiles. The eyetooth on his left side is only half its proper length and torqued.

She blinks. He leans a little closer, confides: "World of wonders on the other side." He smells of lemon. He smells of chewed hay, horse sweat, smoked ham, smoke. Katherine's fingers knot into one another, and now she turns to find the soda girl, who is hopelessly and profoundly unhurried at the counter's other end. Katherine's hands announce her discomfort. She unclasps them, looks forward, toward the mirror, looks back down at the counter again, and feels the man's elbow suddenly high in her side. There are white rays around the man's eyes, lines, and the watches on his vest report vastly different times.

A huckster, Katherine thinks, and she thinks, too, to leave, but the crowd presses from behind, and she hears her mother's heartless voice in her ear: "Don't run from whom you've become. There is no one else to hide with, Katherine. From now on, you're on your own."

Thank you, Mother, Katherine thinks. *You are so kind. You should have seen me for who I have become. You should have asked me what happened. You should have given me the room to be forgiven.*

You should have shown me that you cared.

"World of wonders on the other side," the man says again, meaning Shantytown, Katherine concludes. She hates his rattling voice, the raw flinch and spackle of it. She glances the opposite way, and now as she looks down at the bar she finds herself confronted by a filthy scrap in the huckster's hand—something drawn and distorted, lewd.

"Delicious," the man says, the scribble in his palm. "And not far either. Close by." Bile rises to the back of Katherine's tongue.

"Excuse me," she says.

"Anything you like." He lifts his free hand to Katherine's chin, threatens to touch her, calls her lovely, and after everything, this is the thing that undoes her—this one word, *lovely*, and with her own hand she reaches for his and cuffs it. His skin is like chicken skin. The knuckles on his hands black and bristled.

"A little bit of kick, have you now?" the man says, laughing, putting his lips close toward Katherine's ear. "I like kick. Always fancied it. Thought to myself when I found you here, now—"

But she's loosened her hand from his, and she's turned, facing the crowd, thinking how, if Anna had not done what Anna had done, Katherine would have been spared all this in the first place, the awful red rage of it, the push through the crowd, the sound of the girl at the counter, calling after her now, about the soda.

"Lovely." She hears that word again and now in every angle, mirror reflection, corner, shadow, sunbeam, there is the possibility, no, the probability of her sister's lover. For months Bennett has been seeking Katherine, and Katherine has been spurning him, and there have been letters left, and she will not read them, and she has heard him call her name out on Walnut and she has taken off running.

And there he was, just those few days ago, at the Colosseum. Saving her only because he wants to talk and because she has not yielded. Because he has something to tell her, but what good will it do? He wants her to forgive herself, but why? Katherine is not required to open her heart, not once or ever again. She senses Bennett. She smells him. She lifts her shoulders and lowers her head and through the Centennial crowds she starts walking. Toward the stairs that will lead to the tower that will lead at last to flight.

Eleven

SHE IS BREATHLESS FROM THE CLIMB AND FROM THE VIEW, which renders the Brunswick diamond an undetectable glass mite, the tapping of the telegraph as mute as a pulse.

There is the scent of flour in the air, indisputable and rising.

From where she stands, the spaces in between things look like streets, the rows and rows of American silks like they belong in a department store, and in the benches hunkered down before the music stands whole families wait like congregations for the entertainment to begin.

The organ doesn't sing, it exhales—filling the volume of the Main Exhibition Hall with elaborate moans and peeps. The sound works like a hand in water, sending pulse waves through the minnows below, or at least that is how Katherine, from her perch, has come to see this crowd: as scales and fins, pooling and scattering.

She sees him now.

He sees her.

She turns, but there is nowhere to go.

Not moving as the multitudes pass by, as the elevator

slides, raised up by its bed of steam, its immaculate cables. Not shrinking. This is the future, not the past. This is where the present ends. He will say his piece, be done with it. She will tell him thank you, and seem content to live. He will leave her free, at last. That's the only way out, the only plan. Finally, Katherine understands this.

The fountains beneath Katherine have gone off and died down—a hush and haunt. The telegraph is self-assured, every tap as crisp and right as the last. Through the stained-glass windows the sun has come, thin rays of red and blue that press a shine down hard upon things.

Bennett has begun to move—down the thoroughfares, between the crowds, toward the stairs that will bring him up. She stays where she is.

And yet.

At this very instant, coming toward Katherine in a hurry up the steps, is a young woman Katherine's own age—her eyes alert and alive, her arms encumbered by a baby, her aspect cheery and unguarded. The young woman's costume is the color of blueberries and impeccably modern with its slender collar and shoulders, its complicated cuffs, each finished, Katherine notices at once, with five royal purple buttons and a crisscross of amber thread. It's the sort of dress that Anna would have picked out for herself and paraded about in the upstairs hall, anticipating Bennett's appreciating eye, demanding Katherine's. The sort of dress that Katherine herself would never choose, for it requires an innate confidence in one's own beauty.

"God-awful organ," the young woman proclaims, as if this were any other day, as if Katherine were not in the high ascent of her own final act, and Katherine nods. "Lottie's certainly had her fill." A little out of breath, the color high in her cheeks, the young woman swivels the baby so that Katherine can see the plump face, the ruffled lavender gown. The child has her whole fist pumped into her toothless mouth, the other hand twisted about the young woman's thick-chained necklace. She has no bonnet on her head, only whorls of soft brown hair. The baby is six months old, Katherine guesses. Maybe nine.

"Yours?" Katherine asks feebly, her mouth dry, her head fizzy. She casts her eyes out over the floor, and sees Bennett caught in the clot of people who have come to see the telegraphs work. He is watching her. He is snagged.

"Heavens, no," says the young woman. "My niece. My sister's down there somewhere, lost in Brazil, I imagine. Or Italy. I came up here to scout her out. Lottie thinks it's time for us to find her mother. Don't you, Lottie?"

Lottie's eyes go bigger. The fist remains plunked down in the wet grotto of her mouth.

"Bird's-eye view from up here," Katherine says.

"Something like that. I'm Laura, by the way." She tips forward, for she has no free hand to extend.

"And I'm Katherine."

"You're from here? A Philadelphian?"

Katherine nods. "All my life."

"So you belong here. We're in from Iowa. Iowa," Laura repeats, rolling her eyes. "It's our last night here. Just my sister and me and her daughter. She left her husband at home. Which is good for all of us."

Laura laughs, and when she does, Lottie drags her fist out of the *O* of her mouth, surprising herself with the whopping, sucking sound. *How close is Bennett?* Katherine wonders. *How far?*

Laura turns the baby again and positions her high on her left shoulder, then rotates herself and leans out rather precariously over the rail, scanning the floor below. *Fearless,* Katherine thinks, *like Anna. Alive.* "I wonder where she's gone to," she says. "My sister, I mean."

Katherine turns and peers out, too, over the exhibits, the crowds, the spaces in between—leans far out, like a less cautious person would, and the truth is, she does not see Bennett; the crowd has consumed him. Strange, she thinks, and she doubts herself, doubts the tricks her own mind has played on her since Anna's dying—the in-and-out of the past, the relentless remorse.

"Look at that bright red hat," Laura says now. "The one with all the feathers." Katherine scans the crowd and stops her eyes at the music stand, where five or six women in wheeled chairs have rolled in and a whole phalanx of people press behind. A mass of Chinese men have appeared at the front, their strange hats and black hair stirring a slight commotion, but the biggest commotion arises from the tower of red on the head of a woman who seems, from this distance, to stand some six feet tall.

"I could use a sarsaparilla soda water," Laura sighs. "I think I'll miss those most when I'm gone. Not the technology, but the fizz." She closes her eyes and smiles, as if conjuring the sweet drink. "I will not, however, miss the oysters," she says, wrinkling her nose. "Do you chew them, or just let them slide?" Lottie snivels and Laura gives her a bounce. The baby whimpers and Laura changes shoulders, and suddenly Katherine will do anything on behalf of this new, impossible friendship.

"I could watch her," Katherine offers, but is this what she wants? Taking this child on? Holding on for a while more?

Laura turns and looks searchingly at Katherine. "You would do that? Really?" The baby has dropped her grip on the necklace in favor of her young aunt's chin, which she's pawing with her fist. A bead of sweat makes its way past Laura's ear, and now sits ready to plummet down the pale cavern of her neck.

"I have rather had my fill of the exhibition," Katherine says, her voice sounding strange to herself, "and I prefer the view from up here. Besides," she says, touching the back of Lottie's head, smoothing her dress, "your niece seems in need of a new variety of entertainment. All this stuff"—and Katherine gestures toward the exhibition hall—"is just so much stuff after a while. Even a child can see that."

Laura looks from Lottie to Katherine and back. She glances down across the exhibition hall, as if scanning the floor one last abject time for her sister. "Actually," she says, "it doesn't sound like a terrible idea. If you'd be willing, I'd be grateful."

"I'd be willing," Katherine says.

Laura gives Katherine one more long look, then fits her hands beneath the tiny cups of Lottie's arms. Katherine reaches and suddenly Lottie is hers—a warm, damp weight and two scrunched-up, needy fists. Katherine moves the child about until she fits in her arms. Laura reaches in and smoothes the child's dress.

"I won't be gone long. And if you need me—if she fusses—just come and find me. You'll be able to see me from here."

"We'll be fine. I'll walk her about a bit. Keep her distracted. Take her upstairs, to the rooftop, for the broader view."

"Let me give you something. Get you—"

"You'd take the fun out of it for me. Really, you would. We'll just go and have a look around. We'll meet again, right here. Five o'clock?"

"You're the nicest Philadelphian I've met all week long."

Katherine laughs. "There are others," she says. "Honestly."

Laura smiles. "You be good now, Lottie," she says, touching her finger to the child's miniature nose. The baby squirms and kicks out her feet. She starts to fuss, and Katherine moves her from one arm to another, adjusts her grip. "She's got a mind of her own," Laura warns.

"Well, that makes three of us."

"Do you want anything? Are you sure you don't?"

"I'm sure."

"Five o'clock, Katherine," Laura says, putting a lilt at the end of Katherine's name, a near question. "Right here at the turn of the stairs. I promise." And then: "Thank you."

Glancing back over her shoulder, Laura takes long strides toward the steps. Then she turns, straightens her shoulders, and smoothes her hands across her blueberry costume. Lottie kicks her little cotton-swathed feet. "Now, now," Katherine says, but Lottie squeals. Katherine resettles her, but the child protests again.

"Mind of your own, is that it?" Katherine says gently. "What do you say to a change of view?" Bundling the bobble of heat even closer, Katherine steps toward the uprising stairs, where others are headed—all afternoon they've been headed—to get the rooftop view of the Centennial grounds, of Philadelphia, of the world, as far as it will yield. The elevator slides by them, and Katherine doesn't care;

she climbs. Pressing against Katherine's chest, Lottie waves her tiny clenched fists. Sometimes her face rubs against Katherine's.

"What do you think so far?" Katherine whispers into the child's ear, midway up the stairs. She feels a warm wet tear begin to fall from her right eye, her lungs sobbing for air within her chest, something going weak in her arms. Lottie gurgles her approval. Katherine places a kiss upon her cheek and refuses to glance back over her shoulder. Bennett will find her soon enough. Bennett will come, but she has Lottie.

"Wait until we get to where we're going," Katherine promises, and now Lottie laughs a brilliant, hiccuping laugh, as if she's already imagining the wonders of the view, as if she has it within her power to keep her keeper safe.

Twelve

At the top of the steps, Katherine turns and finds Bennett, taller than she remembers, his eyes searching hers. After so much running, Katherine simply yields; she will not be chased any farther. He is a beautiful man, not a handsome one. It hurts to stand here and see him.

"A baby?" Bennett asks, leaning in close, forcing her to lean closer to him.

"A friend's baby," Katherine says.

He smells of strawberries and yeast, of a long city day, of leftover flour. He looks vastly ruined in the sky space of his eyes. At the funeral he'd worn his father's overcoat, had stood there, ravaged, no one beside him, an only child like Katherine is now an only child; both of them chilled through. Even Katherine, who'd refused to meet his eyes, to acknowledge him at all, could see how violently he was shaking. How sorry he was.

"I saw you at the streetcar stop," Bennett says. "Earlier today."

"You've been chasing me," Katherine says, "for a long time." She shifts Lottie in her arms and stares past Bennett at the accumulating crowd, the too many who have come aloft to get the greater view of Philadelphia, who have never even thought, she's sure, of spreading their wings and flying.

"I wrote you letters."

"I couldn't read them."

"I waited for you in the square."

She glares at him.

"I understand you better than you think."

"You do *not.*" Suddenly the ache and sorrow, the self-recrimination and regret ball up inside her, rage through. "You *could* not. Not possibly." Her fury is sudden, incisive, but Bennett endures, takes it. He has lost something, too. She won't let that matter. His heart is broken. It's her own heart that she's stuck living with, not his. A long time goes by. Lottie punches out her little fist and Katherine kisses her forehead. She waits for Bennett, and Bennett waits, too, gathering his words.

"There is something you should know," he says finally, his voice falling far below the tenor of the organ, which has tuned itself up and is blasting a song. "Just one thing, Katherine, and you'll never need to see me again. I promise."

"You've made other promises."

"This one will last."

"I don't trust you for a second, Bennett."

"Just listen and I'll leave."

"Anna's gone." Katherine leans toward him now. "You

were there. You let it happen." What she says is not true. She knows it but stands by her words.

"I could not stop what happened from happening," Bennett says as if there's a difference, and with his eyes he asks, *Is there a difference?* and suddenly Katherine imagines that he has chased her all this time, hunted her down, to find out the answer to that question. To be made safe from asking it only of himself. He is a beautiful man, and beauty breaks, and he is broken.

"You stole her from me," Katherine says, and she doesn't mean at the river in February, she means all the days before, the barricaded intimacy, the secrets that Katherine was forced to keep, because, *No, Bennett, if you want to know: no*. Katherine never did confide in her father, never would confide in her mother. Katherine never said, *Anna was in love with that boy who was with her at the river. Anna was in love, and he did not save her. Anna was in love, and I knew it, and I did not save her.* Anna is gone, and this is all that Katherine still can give her—her secret kept, from now through eternity. Katherine and Bennett are the only two people alive who know what sort of love theirs was, and this binds them. Lottie is a warm weight in Katherine's arms. She turns the child to face forward. She looks away from Bennett's eyes.

"Katherine," Bennett says now.

"What?"

He steps closer, for the crowd is behind him, because more people have climbed to this height, as if the real show's up here.

"I couldn't reach her. I tried. I couldn't."

"You didn't love her like I loved her, Bennett. Maybe that's why." And of course that's not why, of course not—he would have saved her if he could have; he wouldn't have lost her, not on purpose; he would have kept her alive, for they would marry someday—wasn't that the plan of it, they'd marry? Anna in immaculate white and Katherine by her side and big-mouthed tulips in every corner of the Church of the Holy Trinity on Rittenhouse Square, and they would have married in spring despite her parents' warning, a wedding, not a funeral, because in the end Anna would have had to tell, and in the end, Pa'd have said yes, because beauty always wins. The fist of this logic sits somewhere in Katherine's brain—Bennett would have never let her sister die, never *allowed* it to happen—but Katherine makes the accusation anyway, spits it out: *murderer*. She'd pound her fists against his chest and make him bring her Anna back, *bring her back, she was my sister*, but it's the two of them and Lottie in this crowd, Katherine's hands momentarily bound up with the child.

"We loved her differently," Bennett says. "But Katherine." His eyes aren't sky. They're clouds and storm.

"I don't know what you want, Bennett. I don't know what I can give you."

"I'm not asking for anything. You're not responsible. . . ." And of all the things Bennett might have said just then, this is the thing that Katherine won't withstand. This is what does her in here, at the Centennial, when she was trying to be so righteously brave. For if Katherine isn't needed for anything, if she is no longer *responsible* for Anna, who is she now? What can she give? He, her sister's lover, has stripped her of this, too. Lottie whimpers, and Katherine turns her to her shoulder. She howls, and Katherine looks far past Bennett; she succumbs to the drowning moan of the organ.

"Her final thoughts were for *you*," Bennett says. "That's it, Katherine. That's all. That's all I wanted you to know." He pulls his fingers through his hair, then touches one finger to Lottie's ear. He looks for Katherine to meet his eyes—just this one time—and Katherine does. Everything shatters. Every last thing.

"What are you saying?" Katherine sobs.

"Your name," he says, "was Anna's last word. The last thing your sister ever said."

"Don't," Katherine says. "Please don't," but he says, "I loved her, too," and now the crowd is coming on, the crowd is pushing in, and Katherine reaches past Lottie, toward Bennett, but he is gone.

Thirteen

There is a long white plume of smoke rising from the Centennial train in the distance. There are crowds everywhere. Katherine has climbed. She has carried Lottie to the highest spot—to this balcony above the city from which, all day, Katherine has imagined soaring, swooping, falling. Bennett is gone now, and Katherine is devastated, holding Lottie tight, telling her to look, to see—see that smoke; see that long strut of Machinery Hall next door; see that procession of windows and steeples, thin as weather vanes; see the future, Lottie. Touch it and take it; it is yours.

But Lottie wants to take in the whole protuberating thing at once. Her head bobs and her fingers fan, and if she could walk, she would; if she could fly—up above Belmont Avenue and the Bartholdi Fountain; above the Glass Magazine and the Torch of Liberty; above Tunis, Chile, Brazil, France, Spain; above the states of the union, the palaces of arts and white gardenia, the Women's Pavilion (for there, in the distance are the glorifying flags and the palace geometries of Mrs. Gillespie's monumental

Women's Pavilion)—it would be so much better. Fly, but never fall.

Far to the west rises the tower of George's Hill, and to the north, the trees and ravines and grass and sky from which this Centennial city has been carved, and when Katherine turns herself and Lottie south, out of the blare of the fat sun, the view is of Elm and of Shantytown beyond, standing on its cheap peg legs. There's a jam of horses, hackneys, four-in-hands, gigs, streetcars at the corner near the Trans-Continental. There's a passel of balloons, the coming and going and stopping of seersucker and serge, of uniforms and skullcaps, of licorice-colored satchels and mahogany canes, of a pale wooden crate of bright yellow flowers, an island unto itself. There are two flour-dusted boys carrying sacks of bread, and the carmine flash of a bold silk hat, and the gleam of Tufts, and the sausage man, and Lottie kicks her little feet and punches her fist. She gurgles and squirms. Katherine lifts the child higher in her arms, gives her as much room as she can so that she might see for the both of them, as much space as can be salvaged among the crowds that have gathered here with them, upon the roof of the main building.

Anna's final thought was of her. Anna's final word was *Katherine.*

"Let's watch," Katherine whispers in the baby's ear, "and see what happens," and while they stand facing south,

Katherine turns her head east and looks out upon the spires, rooftops, bridges, and factories of Philadelphia, her city. The redbrick and white lintels and brownstones and green swaths and temples of home. It is flat-roofed, peaked and pompous, congested and incomplete. Katherine's eyes cannot possibly hold it all, until finally they settle on the dark bracelet of the Schuylkill River, which arrives from the north, pools and calms, before hurrying away with itself. *Cure yourself,* she thinks. *Look away.* But she cannot. Winter returns. February 6. The day she lost Anna.

"Katherine, come with us. Please," Anna is demanding. "It's the only way." But Katherine doesn't turn. It's so bitter cold outside that ice has crystallized the view from their window, so cold in their room that Katherine has pulled the quilt up past her nose, curled her knees toward her chin. She breathes into her cupped hand, using her lungs like a furnace. She stares through the gray light of the room, toward Anna, who has cast her covers off and who stands before the window in her soft green sleeping gown. She wears her feet bare, and her hair, her fantastically unruly hair, rises out above her head like a woolen muff. Immune to the temperature, she traces Bennett's name against the glass with a long, pale finger.

"You'll catch your death of cold," Katherine scolds, yanking her quilt up higher, toward her ears. "Get back into bed."

Downstairs Jeannie Bea is preparing the morning meal—sausage, it seems; eggs; their father's coffee. Katherine can smell the butter as it begins to heat, hear the bang of a spoon against a pan, and now she hears Mother down the hall, buttoning herself into her Sunday suit, no doubt. The same forbidding suit each Sunday, the same stiff hat, the same pair of commonsense boots.

"You're impossible," Anna says.

"And you're like a child."

"Nearly a full moon last night," Anna says. "Didn't you see?"

"I was sleeping," Katherine says.

"But the moon," Anna says, "was huge." She takes two dainty steps toward Katherine's bed and then yanks the quilt straight down—a sudden draft of cold.

"Anna!" Katherine protests. Her eyes are small, swollen ridges of exhaustion.

Anna crawls in, piling the quilt on top of them both.

"I could sell you," Katherine says, "as ice." Despite the abhorrent blast of arctic air, she laughs into her sister's hair, which has massed itself over her pillow like lost spring vines.

"They could sell you as coal," says Anna. "Kindling. You'd make someone a fortune."

"I'll make my own fortune someday, thank you."

"Don't start. You'll sound like Mother."

Katherine shudders, and Anna laughs, and for a moment

they lie there taking the heat and the cold from each other until finally Katherine's warmth wins out.

"Mother's going to insist on church," Katherine says. "I've heard her getting ready."

"We'll go, and I'll be perfectly well behaved," Anna says. "I'll sing the hymns, say my hellos. Give a nod to Alan Carver."

"Your Mr. Carver's found his match," Katherine reminds her, though of course she doesn't need to, of course it was scandalous the way Anna carried on, flouting the poor man at every turn until finally—it took a laughably long time—he dispensed with her, too, showing up at the Academy one evening with Sophia Crawford on his arm—Sophia, with her leonine face and unavoidably colossal nose.

"Poor Sophia," Anna says, but Katherine knows she doesn't mean it.

"Mother will want us home for Sunday lunch," Katherine cautions. "Mrs. Gillespie herself is coming for tea. Or so Mother hopes. She's in a buzz about it. She's made her plans."

"We'll be home for Sunday lunch. Bennett can't even get away until late afternoon. Before sunset. That's what he said. 'I'll meet you there sometime before sunset.'" When, Katherine wonders, had these particular plans been set? These lovers' promises? She thinks of the last time she saw them out on Walnut Street together—their hats pulled low across their faces, their heads bent against the wind.

To anyone but Katherine they would have seemed anonymous, indistinguishable from the rest of the passersby in a city where winter had finally come, after so many days of a strange January thaw. Two people in a hurry on a Friday afternoon, taking care not to be seen. Katherine tried desperately not to see them. She doesn't want to see them now, but still: she's been invited to the river.

"What will you tell them this time? What excuse will you give?" Katherine props herself up on one elbow and looks down on Anna, who schemes with her eyes closed and seems blissfully unconcerned with the secret she's perpetuated, the lies she's grown so expert at telling. Into the cave of the quilt the cold air flows, and now Katherine settles down again, pulling the quilt over both their heads and huffing warmth into her hands. Anna murmurs.

"We'll make it mysterious," she says. "On purpose. Make Mother think that our going out has to do with her birthday."

"That's not for two weeks!"

"Well. One has to plan."

"You're awful."

"Come on, Katherine. Please. It's the first time the river's been frozen all winter."

"Mother doesn't care about her birthday," Katherine interrupts. "It's not a very reliable plan."

"You come up with something, then."

"Why should I?"

"Because I'm irresistible, that's why."

"So you've said. A million times."

"Because the river's frozen and the moon is so full. Because you love to skate even more than I do. Because you're good at it."

"Not skating alone. I'm not good at that."

"But you won't be alone, Katherine. Bennett will be there. Me too."

Katherine can't help it: she groans. "You must be kidding, Anna. I'm always alone when you're with Bennett."

"Oh, Katherine!" And now Anna is up on one elbow, looking genuinely aggrieved. "I thought—"

"We said we wouldn't talk about it anymore, and honestly, I don't want to." Katherine turns toward the wall and brings her knees back up toward her chin, remembering Cape May and the months after Cape May, the week neither spoke to each other. Anna had never confessed about Bennett to Father; in the end, after making her promise, she'd refused. Katherine had threatened; she had ridiculed. She had called her sister a narcissist, a burden, and that's when Anna had left her, in the park, one afternoon. "I don't need you," Anna'd growled, and that was it, and from then on, for days, she behaved as if she didn't—making her own plans and telling her own lies, taking her own risks, which she would not speak of later. Telling Katherine nothing, for Katherine had lost her.

Katherine was the one, as it turned out, who was in desperate need of a sister, the one who could not survive without. By October, Katherine understood that she had this choice: either settle her debts with her sister, or lose her altogether. There could be no more fighting about Bennett. No more accusations, either way. Katherine would not press against promises once made. She would leave Anna and her lies and her Bennett be, for the return of at least some fraction of Anna's heart.

It was colder, Katherine realized, on her left side, facing the thick plaster wall. It was always colder, turned away. Now beyond them, in the hall, she hears their mother's boots stomp by. There's the bristle of suit skirts, a pedantic sigh.

"Girls," their mother calls. "We're leaving by nine."

"I was only saying that you're not alone," Anna whispers. "And you brought it up, besides." She touches a hand to Katherine's right shoulder and applies pressure. Katherine succumbs—turns and falls, lies flat on her back, her eyes on the small gas lamp by the door frame.

"We're not talking about it," Katherine whispers back. "I'm not, anyway." Anna sighs. She relaxes back down to the pillow so that her hair spills out in most directions—long, loose, unmanageable curls. Lengths of it graze across Katherine's cheek. She brushes them aside.

"Girls!" It's their mother again, calling up to them from the base of the stairs, then calling out to Jeannie Bea. "Mrs. Gillespie," she says, then something about cheese.

"You're probably right," Katherine says after a while, "about the river. It could be the last freezing all winter."

"You'll go then?" Beneath the quilt Anna reaches for Katherine's hand and squeezes it tight.

"I will, but no lies."

Anna waits.

"We'll just tell Mother the truth, is all. We'll say we're going to the river to skate. If Bennett comes, well then, he comes. But at first it will only be us."

"Oh," Anna says, "that's lovely." She kisses Katherine on the cheek. "Maybe you'll teach me one of your tricks."

"My tricks," Katherine echoes, and she feels herself grow warm with pride.

"Girls!" Their mother's voice trumpets up the stairs.

"Katherine? Anna?" Now their father joins in, and if they're not careful, Jeannie Bea will be next, carrying their generously peppered eggs to them on two white, gleaming dishes.

"Coming!" Anna answers. She yanks at the quilt, and the cold scorches them both. Scorches Katherine, anyway. Anna's too intoxicated with the promise of the coming afternoon to notice.

* * * *

Before they even see the Schuylkill they hear the skaters' shouts. Their father has sent them off with George, his favorite hansom driver, and with a dark horse named Hank who blows dragon steam through his nostrils. The horse kicks at the stony streets whenever George tries to rein him in. He pulls hard against the turns, throwing the twins against each other. Under a wool blanket they sit, their steel skating blades clinking steadily upon their laps. Mrs. Gillespie had remained long after she had finished her second cup of ginger tea and the wedge of Brie that Jeannie Bea had baked beneath crumbles of cinnamon sugar. The talk had been of monies raised, of a building in progress, of regrets over the choice of architect, of *priorities*, and their mother had been (Anna was the one to say so) extraordinarily pleased with herself. "Look at her," Anna had insisted behind her hand. "It's as if she has found her first friend."

"Be home before dark." That was their mother's final instruction before they left for their skating afternoon, though she barely turned her head so as not to disturb the tea with her venerable guest, who was, by the way, not distinguished in person—not, at least, in Anna's whispered estimation. She had mock-curtsied, Anna had—in the hall, spreading all her skirts, unseen by anyone but Katherine or Jeannie Bea, who had covered her smile with a long-practiced hand.

You're terrible, Katherine had meant to tell her, but now

their father was there by the door, holding out to each a muff, which he promptly hung about their necks, Anna's first. "I've asked George to wait and bring you back," he told them. "But don't take advantage of him. Please. It's frigid cold. It's Sunday. Let him come home before dark."

Anna had stretched onto her toes to kiss their father high on the cheek. She had fit her gloved hands inside the flecked muff, then pulled them out again so that she might carry her own pair of blades, which Katherine had collected from the closet. "Thank you, Father," she said, and meant it, and Katherine found herself yearning again that there had never been a Bennett—for her own sake, for the protection of their father, and for the sake of honesty.

They were gone after that—tucked in behind George and his impatient Hank, watching the familiar streets through the small squares of glass. Past the square. Up north. Toward Spring Garden Street. Out west. The streets being more or less empty, for it was Sunday and cold, and it was that hour in between things, when people sat with their Bibles on their laps, or the news in their hands, or their schoolbooks beside the gas lamps in their parlors. When people sat after a Sunday meal, a hymn in their heads.

The girls can hear the intrepid skaters through the square glass of George's cab—the high hollers and pitched calls of winter revelers on a river that had refused to freeze until now. The girls are past the dam, on the east side of the reservoir and the Water Works, where the pavilion stands tall over the steep rock garden and yields an impeccable view. They are around the corner, coming onto Boathouse Row. Hank, reluctantly, is being reined in. The journey's over. George is calling to the girls through the trapdoor. "Here we are then. You've picked quite a day for it." Far away, in the effervescent winter sky, the moon has begun to ascend.

"We're here," Katherine says. Beneath the blanket Anna squeezes her sister's gloved hand until George's face appears in the scratchy glass. When he opens the door, he offers his arm—to Katherine first, then Anna. He has a craggy face and tender eyes. His hair is long and gray-blond beneath a crushed hat.

"Brisk, isn't it?" he says as a blast of wind rushes by and catches in Katherine's ear.

"Glorious," Anna answers, pulling a scarf down tighter over her hair.

"Someday I'll get my own blades and join you on the river," George warns them.

"Oh, you should," Anna tells him. "Skating is lovely."

"Hank needs a little stabling," George says. "We'll go do our business and be back before sundown. You two make the most of it now, will you?" He blows warm air into his thinly gloved hands, then digs them both into his deep pockets.

"Take as long as you like," Anna says, smiling.

"I promised your father," George tells her, and she nods.

From where they stand, the sisters see a game being played out on the river—two groups of boys whooshing a silver pail between them with sticks, one team wearing maroon scarves about their necks. The girls and women tend to hover near the river's shore, or drift out farther, west and north. One girl in a gray-blue coat is sailing out and fast away on a diagonal, her coattails lifting up and flapping behind, revealing a skirt made entirely of summer yellow. With her shoulders pressed forward and her blades pushing her on, she seems intent on vanishing.

"Where do you suppose she's going?" asks Anna.

"Perhaps to Birdsboro," Katherine guesses as they move across the frozen earth toward the frozen ice. "Or Valley Forge." But just as Katherine predicts a long journey for the skater, the girl performs a miraculous pivot and begins to sail toward the shore, lifting one leg behind her as she does and holding herself up like an *L*, on an assured leg, causing one of the boys with the stick and the scarf to stop and stare. He hollers for her then and others do, too, and she remains intrepid above the steady foot on the frozen body of the Schuylkill. There are cheers. Applause that would be so much louder if it weren't for the muffs and gloves.

Katherine is the first to find her balance. She remembers not to walk the ice but to float across, continuous. The river is a million shades of ice—the silver nitrate of a daguerreotype, the veining of white marble, the delicate fiberwork of a spinner's weave, with sticks and bits of things stuck in. It is the reflection of sky, of the Water Works, of the boathouses, of the Philadelphia Skating Club and Humane Society flag that flies above, on the eastern shore. The boys with the bucket are farther down toward the dam, and the acrobatic girl has sought refuge temporarily—glided off the river onto the tundra beyond, where she can be confused with anybody else, except when her coat reveals her yellow skirt.

Now Katherine hears Anna calling her name from the bank; she skates back to collect her. Anna's muff is precisely like Katherine's—the soft fur of a rabbit—but she wears hers like jewelry, and her hair tumbles from the scarf about her head enchantingly unruly. But she becomes instantly comedic when she tries to skate. Already her ankles and knees are buckled in, her elbows are crooked, she has that look of sweet terror on her face. Taking one small, tentative step toward Katherine, Anna skids precipitously. Katherine is right there to catch her.

"Is it always this slick?" Anna wants to know, and Katherine laughs.

"Only where there's ice," she answers.

"Somehow," Anna says, "I'd forgotten." She opens the wing of her arm and, releasing her hand from the muff momentarily, Katherine slips her own arm into the open space. Anna makes a tiny, pedaling effort with one foot, nearly loses her balance, charms her way out of disaster.

"You'll have to do better than that," Katherine tells her, struggling to find a balance that suits the two of them.

"Just take me with you," Anna says. "Until I get the feel of the ice beneath my feet."

"Drag you about, you mean?"

"Not for long, Katherine. Only until I get my footing."

"All right, then," Katherine says, leaning into the cold wind and pressing into the ice with her blades. Soon the blades edge in and slowly the two draw away from the bank, where a new family has arrived, a few more boys to play the bucket game, an older woman who is being pushed about on a bladed chair by a man who seems much younger. Anna tries to keep up with Katherine, periodically punching her blade tip to the ice for balance. *Like a whirligig,* Katherine thinks, and smiles, for the truth is she has her sister precisely where she likes her best—at her side and in her debt. The Humane Society men are here, piling the accoutrements of rescue along the river's edge and gliding about with their reels of twine.

It's a magnificent sky—big enough for both the sun and moon, a virgin blue but for whiskered patches of gray. Up on Lemon Hill, all but the pines and spruces are bare. On the river itself, Katherine sees places where the sun seems to come from down below, beaming up through caves of slumbering fish and bearded shells. Beside Katherine, Anna has regained her equilibrium, her natural grace. She wonders out loud whether Bennett will come.

The acrobatic girl has returned to the ice. The boys have grown tired of their sticks and silver pail and form a loose circle around the girl, who is whipping herself into dizzying spins. She begins with her feet spaced far apart and her arms out before her, as if she is hugging a tree. And then somehow she pulls her feet and arms in, and it is in this way that she accumulates speed.

"I'd have to go be sick," Anna says, for Katherine has steered the two of them toward the crowd and is studying the mechanics of the two-footed spin so that she might try it later, perhaps next Sunday, if the weather holds. Suddenly Katherine has visions of spending all February and March like this: Sundays at the river with her sister. Sunday in the blaze of this rare happiness.

"I hope he's all right," Anna says. "Bennett, I mean."

"Of course he is, Anna. What could happen?"

Anna looks as if she might actually consider answering the question, but Katherine preempts the possibility, pointing to the crowd, where one of the boys with the maroon scarf has joined the girl who spins, and they now stand, facing each other. The daredevils cross arms, hold hands, pump their legs, lean back, and when they finish the whip of their doubled-up spin, their spectators holler, urge them to do it again. The second time they spin, the boy's scarf unwinds itself—lifts off like a bird, falls to the ice, and skids, causing a blot of boys to yammer after the prize. Clawing at one another, the boys fall upon themselves, until the smallest one, himself hatless and tousled, rises victorious and holds the scarf above his head like a battle flag.

Now the wind kicks in from the east, and the boy puts his hands to his ears, and of course he has made his flag severely vulnerable. Within moments, he loses his prize to an outstretched hand, and now a chase is on—the boys; the girl, too; all of them after one another.

The wildness fractures and weaves past the twins to the south, then circles around, howling, bawling, battering, splitting the group into two separate chases that zag out—one west, the other north. It is from within this chaos that Anna unlocks her arm and pulls away. It is now that Katherine feels the tug and absence. She looks east, and when she finally gains perspective through the rumple of the dissipating crowds, she sees Bennett, his eyes like the blue heart of a fire. If his wool coat strains across his shoulders, if his sleeves fall short, if his scarf is splitting along its edges, if he is still and only a baker's boy, a baker himself now, a life chosen for him, Katherine concedes his beauty. He moves easy and loose and unconcerned with how he might be seen or who might be watching as he slides toward Anna, who stands perfectly still on her own two feet, her arms outstretched. Instinctively Katherine steps aside, and when the lovers embrace she understands that she exists no more, not to Bennett, not to Anna. The wind bristles in Katherine's ear. If she tries to swallow, she will harm herself. She will not recover. She will die.

"You've come!" Katherine hears Anna's voice up against Bennett's collar.

"I said I would."

He takes half a step back and tucks a stray strand of Anna's hair into her scarf and looks the way he looks into her eyes—as if all the beauty in the world is Anna, as if the world itself is Anna. Katherine's loneliness is complete, and there is no choice in this: survival means striking the two lovers from her mind. It means leaving now, no warning.

The skater with the yellow skirt has retreated to the bank. She is teaching a young girl in a cherry-colored coat to spin.

"Tell me how you do it," Katherine asks her. "Please?" She has waited until the skater has grown idle; she has kept her distance until now. She has to call out twice for the girl to hear her, and when she finally turns, the skater fixes her eyes on Katherine and smiles.

"Hello," she says. She'd be an ordinary-seeming girl, except for her eyes, which are stoked and bright. She's tied her walnut-colored hair behind her in a loose knot. Her cheeks are red. Her coat is old, Katherine can see from up close—missing a button and patched on one sleeve. Still, Katherine envies her and makes no secret of it.

"You're the best I've ever seen," she says. "I wonder at how it all gets done."

The girl's smile widens. Her lips are chapped and slightly green-blue. "My mother," she says, "was a skater. She taught me everything. You just have to give in to it, and when you do, it's easy."

"I'd give anything to spin like you do," Katherine confesses.

"You could if you'd like."

"But how does it happen?"

"Speed," the skater says. "Power. Balance." She cocks her head, and Katherine sees how her teeth are crooked and her face is freckled, and how altogether she makes a striking picture.

Katherine considers: Speed. Power. Balance.

Beyond them another game has started up with the silver pail; it hisses and hollers across the ice. The older woman on the bladed chair has been pushed toward the river's edge, where she sits like a spectator watching the girl in the cherry-colored coat practice the lesson she's been given. Girls skate with girls, and boys with girls, and husbands and wives with each other, while the Humane Society men lean into the wind, clasping their gloved hands behind their backs, blowing frosted *O*s out of their serious mouths. The sky has changed again; the sun is lower. The river is dusted with shavings of ice, scribbled into, bruised; the light seems to have gone out from it.

The skater is coming toward Katherine, arms outstretched. "It isn't that hard," she says, "once you get the knack of it."

She takes Katherine's hands into her hands. Her grip is strong. She strokes toward an empty place, and Katherine glides beside her. "I'm Katherine, by the way," she says.

"Oh," the skater laughs, "I'm Elizabeth. But most people call me Lizzy."

It's a good name, Katherine decides at once. She breathes and it doesn't hurt as much. She swallows, and she's still alive.

"Think of stretching your arms around a huge patch of sky," Lizzy begins. "And then of pulling the sky in hard, against your heart." Lizzy takes several quick strokes in a straight line, does something with one foot, holds out her arms. "Like this," she shouts. "Like this. You see?" Her coat kicking up, her summer skirt whirling.

It turns out not to be so very hard. Speed, power, balance, the sky pulled toward the heart—she'd never be able to explain it to another, but it works somehow, an alchemical mix that blurs Katherine's edges and gives her a fizzing, fuzzed-out feeling. She's taken her muff off and moved it out of the way, she's untied the scarf from about her neck, and she's gone at it again and again, until she's strong enough on her own for Lizzy to join her, and now side by side they spin, collecting a small audience of their own. Whenever she stops, she feels dizzy, but then she starts again, and even one of the men from the Humane Society has taken himself off duty so that he might admire the spinning skaters.

The moon and the sun have become the same thing. Katherine can't tell one from the other, and she doesn't care, and when she hears the shouting from far away, near the dam, she assumes it's another game of chase and spins on and on. It's Lizzy who finally touches her arm. "Katherine?" she says. The startle of a question.

"Yes?"

"Katherine, do you hear that?"

"What?" But now she does. Now she's steadying herself, separating north from south, sky from ice, moon from sun. She's aware of the bedlam of skaters scuttling toward the dam; of the Humane Society rescuers racing to the banks for their poles and hooks, racing back out again, south; and of how all this while the panic on the river grows, the desperate cries of those who wish to help, and sure as the heart that is beating in her chest clangs on, Katherine knows. Katherine calls her sister's name: "Anna! Anna! Anna!" She screams it, she screams the name.

Lizzy wrenches her arm, and they go—flying not skating over their blades, calling out cautions to any gang, clot, cluster in the way, and knot after knot unties itself to give the two room to tunnel through toward the dam, where a patch of ice has given way and Bennett is on his knees, prostrate.

No, Katherine thinks. *No. This cannot be*, and her legs beneath her slide, and she cannot breathe, and Lizzy, beside her, wrenches her arm again, yanks her up short, warns, "Katherine, look: the ice is cracking. We cannot go any farther." Pointing with her free hand to the skeins of splinters that blast their way across the ice, the fractures and snaps of distress.

"But it's my sister," Katherine pleads, pounds at those who lock her in. "My Anna." She fights Lizzy, but Lizzy will not let her go, the men from the Humane Society will now not let her go, the crowd wedges itself up against her—*You'll fall, too; you'll drown; you watch yourself*—and they are dragging Bennett from the ice-patch edge, holding their poles over the dark, running current, unreeling their twine. They are shouting, "Stand back," and waving their arms, and now here is George beside Katherine, smelling of horses and wool, a pint of beer; George in his boots, looking immensely terrified; George who will never set foot again on a river.

"It's Anna," Katherine says, and she collapses into him.

"My Anna." Her legs leave her. Her strength. By strangers and a horseman, she is held aloft while the rescue men pole and dig and reach. While Bennett stands there, frantic.

Katherine feels the kick in her gut and knows it's Lottie. She feels the elbows now of the Centennial crowd, the push and grab of strangers on a roof beneath a vanishing sun, the day moving on, past itself. "But do you see that?" she hears someone say, and when she glances toward Shantytown, she sees the spire of a flame.

Fourteen

The first flames poke through the raw-boned roof of C. D. Murphy's Tavern like the ears of a tabby cat, a striping of ocher and black that keeps to itself at first, prowling and small. "But do you see that?" the stranger repeats, and by the time Katherine understands that it is not some Centennial spectacle being ogled but a fire across Elm, others have got the story, too. The sun is playing its duplicitous tricks, and all about the Centennial grounds shoals of people—one hundred thousand in all—move saturated, stupefied. "But do you see that?" Katherine turns, and just then the fire leaps high and begins to waggle west. In a day of wonders it seems but another one, a shameless curiosity, but right as Katherine has this thought, the fire doubles up on itself and cleaves. Lottie sees it. Lottie punches out her fist and grabs at the nearest hunk of sky.

Down below, in the jumble of Elm, gawkers have arrived, sudden evictees, porters, a tall man in plaid pants, a collection of waiters, a crowd of children running ahead of their mothers. Some of the horses in their harnesses are rearing back, bucking to rid themselves of the weight of the carriages for which they've been responsible all day. "The engines are coming," someone says, but Katherine's eyes are on the insolent, fast-raging fire, which does not burn in place but keeps on multiplying, pushing its tongue through more burst windows of Shantytown now, as its victims pour onto Elm. One of the hansom cab horses has taken off on his own, his driver galloping behind.

The fire burns in place, seems to consider. It maintains its hold on the east, drops a final curtain on two saloons, blackens Theodore Bomeisler's hotel, puts an end to Ullman's eatery. It turns the sky to smoke and now arrives at the door of the Ross House, which is sturdy brick, not wood, four stories high, and where the boarders are working their own rescue like bees in a hive, tossing through windows their trunks, their bedsheets, their instruments of beauty, their twelve-cent *Ledgers*, as if they cannot bear to leave the news behind. *Leave the news be*, Katherine thinks, *the news is dead.*

Now come paired men and a woman with a trundle bed between them; a ransomed velvet chair; a settee with carved swan's feet and dimpled, upholstered hearts; a gilt frame; a pail of brushes and an artist's palette. Men and women who seem to have stripped the Oriental runners from the stairs within, who seem determined to go nowhere without a corset box, an umbrella stand, a pair of candlesticks. The Ross House cooks stagger about in the streets with their arms clasping blackened cooking pots, soup tureens, porcelain platters, dessert bowls. The salvaged and the salvagers have no discernible plan, and now the fire brigade has come in, and river water pounds from all directions—hard, white, spitting streams.

The wind is at the fire's back. It leaps and dazzles and still more boxes are being thrown to the street, and suddenly from one narrow doorway emerges a giantess in a tented dress—the famous fat woman of Shantytown, Katherine realizes—who seems surprisingly fleet on elephantine feet. Elm is all at fever pitch. Elm has been infiltrated, and now the Centennial police have arrived, their whistles shrill above the melee, above the boom of the fire leaping higher.

In Katherine's arms, Lottie has begun to cry, and when Katherine turns to see the throng behind her on the roof, she understands that the world's largest building has exceeded its rooftop capacity. *Thin as ice,* Katherine thinks, pulling Lottie even closer, pulling her straight to her heart.

She would cry for Laura, but Laura won't hear. Laura is somewhere down below, and right now, right in this instant, again, Katherine is alone with her terrible responsibility.

Now across the bedlam alley, the final roof timber of C. D. Murphy's falls. The brigade of amateur firefighters has begun its fight—unblenched paladins armed with buckets and basins of slosh. One man is throwing bricks at the conflagration, as if he could break its neck, but there's too much summer heat in brittle Shantytown. In most every direction there is the crepitating *pop* of structure giving way, advertisements in a peel on the smudged faces of the shops, the startling demise of cheap curtains, the shattering of lanterns.

"More brigade on its way," a woman yells, a chambermaid, three brooms in her hands, a mop, as if these were the lives most worth saving. Katherine strains and suddenly she sees William with his wheat-colored hair and the sand-colored mutt, down on the ground, near the tavern where this fire first began. Together they run, and now Katherine sees William stop outside Allen's Animal Show, where a counting pig and a notorious cow are kept, birds in cages, a pair of titanic sea cows. Everyone knows this. Everyone's read it. William seems to have taken it to heart.

He pounds at the door and lets himself in. He disappears, and the fire is raging; the fire is coming, Katherine realizes, for him, and her heart stops at the thought, her lungs go airless.

When the mutt emerges from the flames he is unrecognizable soot—dancing on his hind legs. A cat breaks through the flaming door of Allen's. A collie breaks free of its own rope collar and leaps, teeth bared, onto Elm.

The walls of Allen's are crumbling. The ceiling is collapsing into embers, and right then, through the almost-nothing of the building that was, a bird comes fluttering free, her wings *thwack-thwack*ing within the grim-gray smoke, a broken chain dangling down from one webbed foot. Katherine remembers Operti's, the girl with the bird, is suddenly brokenhearted at the possibility of them coming to harm. Where is the girl? Where is the bird? She watches the unchained dove float all the way up through the smoke toward the sky. The fire burns in place and then, with a new ferocity, it launches, again, toward virgin territory, until the entire alley is flame and fury and finally William appears, black-faced and stumbling, alive.

Alive, Katherine thinks. And it's the most beautiful word that there is.

The fire is white at its most true. It is yellow, orange, smoke, and plasma in the blistered rags above its heart. It will burn harder with the wind, and like a fish caught in a net, Katherine cannot move. She cannot free herself to return Lottie to Laura. She cannot find the stairs or make her way to the street. She cannot join William in whatever mission he has set for himself, for it is clear to Katherine that he has set out for himself the task of saving things, of rescue.

There is so much pressure at Katherine's back that she cannot so much as turn to glance over her shoulder, to check just in case Laura has, by some miracle, come, but how could Laura come? What was their promise? Five o'clock, at the balcony, on the stairs—an impossible promise. There's no more getting up to the roof now than there is getting down; there's nothing to do but hold Lottie safe, this little girl who has grown warm-damp now, whose hair is lying flat against her face. A bright pink is flourishing on Lottie's face, and she has begun the sort of hiccuping cry that Katherine does not know how to cure.

Beneath her feet the roof feels thin.

Down on Elm, the fire's evictees keep streaming—through doorways, from alleys, out of the dark into the blazing light, some of them forming a battering ram that seems intent on knocking the Centennial turnstiles down. They want in to the Centennial grounds. To the lakes and the fountains and the miracles of the exhibition, to the seeming safe haven on the north side of Elm. Against the gates they press, against the keepers, who have wakened from the somnolence of the afternoon. No one will be let in, no one let out, until the fire dies, until somebody can kill it. "The second brigade is coming," someone says, and now the Centennial police are barricading, holding the terrified masses back. The engines must be let through to do their work. Their horses are frightened and rearing.

The roof deck quails. Katherine feels the simple shudder of the grand construction beneath her feet, she hears the creaking of bolts and screws, and all of a sudden she is deluged by an awful premonition. One tight thing will go loose. One isolated beam will wrangle free. The roof will yield. Into the unhinged jaw of the Main Exhibition they will fall—through folderol, corsets, crockery, engines, fizz, the hard white light of the perfect jewel, through Brazil and Spain and Norway.

Without choosing to fall, they will fall. Lift. Drag. Thrust. Gravity.

Even the future can vanish.

Smithereens, Katherine thinks. *No air.* And now she remembers Anna, thinks as she has tried so desperately hard never again to think of Anna in the suck-down of the Schuylkill, between the teeth of ice. It happened all at once, Bennett said, at the river that day, before his hand could reach hers. It happened. There was the sound of something giving way, a white shattering, and she was gone. Under and into the lick of the winter current, over the dam and down, trapped in the bend and stiff, floating above the cobbled backs of turtles, the hibernating congregations of fish, the undredged leaves and sticks, the slatternly remains of a she-dog. Three days later a boy found Anna at the mouth of the Delaware, her muff still hung about her neck.

"There, there." It's the woman beside Katherine, who smells like bratwurst, whose scored and dimpled neck is as thick as a club. She chucks a finger the size of a thumb under Lottie's chin, and if Lottie stills for one abrupt instant, the corresponding scream is power. She shakes and tosses off the touch of the stranger's finger, and Katherine shifts her, kisses her forehead.

"It's all a bit much," Katherine says, and again Lottie screams, she grows inconsolable. She has become an exhausting weight in Katherine's arms, kicking a hole in the sky.

"I'll say it's much," the woman harrumphs. "They've got us like prisoners up here." The knot at the back of the woman's head has come undone, and chunks of auburn hair fall gracelessly forward. Her eyes are small and deep in the full yellow moon of her face, and now Katherine looks past her, to the man on her left, who seems transfixed by the spectacle of fire. Ash bits waft through the air like confetti. There's the taste of char on Katherine's tongue.

Lottie wants out. She wants down—her little feet working like pistons so that Katherine has to hold her tight, wrap all her strength around her. "Look, Lottie," she says, for down below the police have finally succeeded in forging a tunnel with the firefighting steamers. This brigade on Elm has turned its back to the fire. They have raised their nozzled hoses to the pert glass face of the Main Exhibition Building, and now they are firing. Someone near Katherine begins to cry. Long, gulping, inconsolable cries.

"It's just a precaution, miss," an old man in a checkerboard vest says as if he's seen plenty of this in his day.

"Bloody ugly fire," a British gentleman says, and a British woman answers, "Wait'll I tell me missus."

The smoke billows and slows. The fire sends bright ribbons up into the sky and seems to begin to lose some interest in itself. Even as the spectators holler, even as the horses stomp, even as the attenuated roof of the Main Exhibition Building twitches, the fire seems to sicken of its own mad greed. It has fallen from the height of its early spires and has divided. It has failed to launch across the processional width of Elm. It has bowed its head in places to the streaming river water. William and his mutt have disappeared. Katherine searches for them. She sends her hope out to meet them. Her hope for rescue. For the return to life.

In Katherine's arms, Lottie is lying perfectly still, asleep now, her face mushed to Katherine's shoulder, her weight sunk against Katherine's slim hip. For the first time she wonders how Laura has done this all day and all week, how mothers do it, and she thinks of her own mother, efficient and brisk, trying to calm twins. It is impossible to remember her mother's touch. Katherine only remembers Anna, the early sweet frustration of confusing her sister with herself.

The sun has fallen. Soon the moon will be on its way. In places, still, the fire is being fought, but even more so now, the fire loses, and there is no more need for the brigade on Elm; the horses are being hitched back to their engines. There is no more need to lock the people in or out; there is the sound of turnstiles clicking. There'll be smoke, Katherine thinks, for days. There'll be the hovering smell of char and ash, but already now some patches of sky are clearing, like a fog rolling off, and between patches Katherine gains a broader view of Elm and Shantytown below, the spoiled victims of the fire, the porters out in the street, the waiters with their fistfuls of silverware, one cook with a bloody back of beef on a tray. The swappers, vendors, dealers, den masters, chambermaids with pots walk the streets in a daze. The hooligans and harlots. One woman ambulates with a fringed parasol popped high, saunters, almost, among the dazed.

At Katherine's back, some of the pressure eases, as finally some are making for the stairs, drawing themselves back down into that paradise of progress, the industrious songs of machines and fountains, in search of the ones they left behind. "They've got the organ started again," someone claims, but Katherine only hears the sound of the street below, she only keeps looking out upon the mangle and mess of Shantytown. Her hips, her arms, her spine are aching, but Lottie must not wake, Lottie must be kept in her incubated slumber until she is with her aunt again, and Katherine understands that she must stay here, in this one place. That Laura will come looking. That they will be found.

Now something down below pricks Katherine's eye. Some distant strangeness that is even more strange than all that has gone before, and in an instant she understands: it's that mutt. Looking like a wolf or a bear in its mangy, sooted coat, prancing like a circus act at the door of the Trans-Continental Hotel. That mutt. That mutt, alone. Her heart hard-walloping against her chest, Katherine strains to see past the dog, beyond it, to William, who must be near—it is desperately important that William be near. For he rescued that pig from the Chauncers' garden, and he stood beside Katherine at the bakery door, and he was there—he was there—before Katherine abandoned her sister. He is part of her before, a one right thing in a dangerous world.

Past the fire, past the smoke, through the detritus and ruins, she strains to see, up and down, but she sees nothing. Only the mutt trotting in its circle.

"There, there," that woman beside her says. "They're letting us down now, do you see? Everything is fine, the fire's dying. And look at your baby asleep, look at you. What a good girl. Come on down now. Danger's over." She puts a hand on Katherine's shoulder. Katherine doesn't turn.

"No," Katherine says. "No. But thank you." For she has her eyes on that mutt and she won't divert herself this time; she cannot afford, ever again, to stop paying attention. If she has learned anything from Anna's dying, it is vigilance. She will live her whole life forward now, on guard.

The pressure behind her keeps easing. The tarnished sun is gone from the sky. A breeze is bringing evening in, and somewhere high above, the stars have agreed to populate the night, to hang above the hordes below who are desperate for passage over the river, to the city, who are packing streetcars, carriages, cabs, who are giving up and walking home.

Fifteen

"Katherine?" She hears her name now. "Katherine?" And still she doesn't turn, still she's looking down, toward the ruin of Shantytown. She feels Laura's arms sweep about her from behind at the same time—a long kiss on her cheek now, thanksgiving. "You're fine," Laura says. "Both of you are fine."

"I'm sorry," Katherine says, turning. "I didn't mean to lose you. I didn't mean . . ." She looks deeply into Laura's eyes and a sob escapes her—a deep, long sob for all that's happened, all she'll never trust herself to say. She looks down again toward Elm, and now even the mutt is gone.

"You didn't lose me," Laura says, stroking the stray hair from Katherine's face. "A fire started."

"I wanted to show Lottie the world from here. I thought . . ."

"And you have, and I'm sure she won't forget it. Here, Katherine, let me take her from you. She can get so heavy when she's dreaming." Laura reaches in and extracts the child. She squirms and resists, clamps a fist to Katherine's hair, which Laura pries loose with a gentle, practiced hand. "Lottie, Lottie, sweet Lottie," she says, and without ever opening her eyes, Lottie finds the balance in Laura's arms and settles in. The emptying is sudden, unbearable—a cavern erupts. Katherine wraps her arms about herself and holds tight.

"What really happened out there?" Laura asks, swaying slightly, looking out now upon the bedlam, the uncountable losses of Shantytown.

"That fire had a mind of its own," Katherine says. She shudders and wipes her face with her hand, streaking her fist with a layer of soot.

"Oh well, now," Laura says. "Don't we all?" And just as she says it, Lottie rouses—opens her eyes and whimpers.

"She's a good girl."

"You must be exhausted."

"No more than the rest of us. How is your sister?"

"She's beside herself and might not ever forgive me," Laura says, but then she smiles. "I better get back to her now, show her Lottie's fine."

"You'll be fine, too, then?"

"We leave for home tomorrow. And you?"

"Home is just across the river," Katherine says. Lottie's whimper is threatening to turn into a cry. Laura bounces her slightly, but her fussing continues.

"I need to go," Laura says. "But here," she says. She digs a card out of her pocket, an engraved address. "Write me in care of my sister. Write and tell me how you are."

Katherine kisses little Lottie on the softest part of her

head. She kisses Laura's cheek good-bye. She will write, she thinks. She will write, she will hold on, but for now, her arms empty, the rooftop crowd dissipating, fighting free, headed home with their strange tales about the future, she has only one thing left to do, and that is to run—to work herself out of the Main Exhibition Building, and out onto the street, in search of William.

Sixteen

Down on Elm it is char and phosphorescent light. The heat between planks. The splinter pop of barrels. There are ghost faces in the windows that still remain in the ruined shacks of Shantytown—a place built with such haste and consumed inside a single day. On the wing tips of the scattered, dying flames, spirits rise.

Nearly dark, and the throngs of people are headed home, cramming the streetcars and trains, walking side by side over the Girard Avenue Bridge, holding on to each other for dear life. The future has been saved, and always, the future is at risk. Nothing is sure. Nothing is certain.

Alone, Katherine veers too close to the burnt-out side of Elm. She won't go home, she has decided, until she finds William and his mutt, until she knows that in saving others he has also saved himself, as Katherine, too, has been saved that day. By Laura. By Lottie. Yes, by Bennett. *Your name was Anna's last word. The last thing your sister ever said.*

"Anna." Katherine says her sister's name out loud, and suddenly a scene from the past floats in—a scene of the sisters together, before Bennett, before the Centennial, before any one of them had come to harm. A scene that she wants to remember today, and also tomorrow. A scene that is Katherine's to protect.

It is late April, the twins' birthday. Adelina Patti has come to town, and Pa has gotten the girls tickets to the Academy of Music—two seats near the stage. It is a beautiful day turned almost evening. The girls leave for the Academy just after six—Anna in coral pink and Katherine in a dress that is either black or blue, depending on how she chooses to stand in the sinking sun. Jeannie Bea has helped the girls with their hair, Anna lacing a red rose into hers at the very last moment.

"Look at you," Pa has said admiringly, looking up from his dinner, which he is eating alone, for Mother has gone out to a meeting. He looks at them both for a very long time. "You are my beauties," he says. "Happy birthday."

Arm in arm they go, Katherine and Anna. Through the wide front door, down the marble stoop, where Gemma yawns as Anna touches her slender finger to the pink triangle of the dear cat's nose. Now they are headed south on Delancey, and over through the square, where lovers are about, women with children, a large man with a larger cigar. Turning onto Walnut, they stroll. Stopping, they press their faces against the glass-fronted stores, exclaiming over the things they'd buy or wouldn't, for they have time, they have each other, they have everything and cannot know it. Broad

Street is a chaos of horses and streetcars, of vendors, of tin signs. For a moment it looks as if Kiralfy's Alhambra Palace is on fire—its four domes catching the sun and its stained-glass windows alive. To come upon Broad requires an act of faith, and Katherine and Anna are patient, they wait, they stand together taking the wide scene in, Anna not pulling ahead.

"Do you suppose she's already inside?" Anna asks, meaning the great Adelina Patti, the dark-haired opera sensation, now in her thirtieth year. She has sung in Saint Petersburg, Buenos Aires, Paris, London, Italy, Spain, on every important American stage. She sang for the Lincolns after the death of their son. She married a marquis. She sings Rossini, Verdi, Donizetti, Mozart, and if the audience demands it, she will sing her intrepid "Home, Sweet Home," and tonight Katherine and Anna will hear her sing, for they have planned this together; they have planned it for weeks. It is the secret that they have held between them: They will ask the great Adelina to sing them "Home, Sweet Home." Calling out to her, from their velvet seats.

A carriage drawn by two chestnut horses with plumed harnesses discharges the first proper couple of the evening. The gentleman wears a silk hat and a white tie. His wife gathers her elaborate skirt and begins to ascend the wide stairs of the Academy. Someone has already gone ahead and lit the gas lamps, and now as more carriages arrive the

Academy steps are overwhelmed, and Broad Street becomes a tide. Anna and Katherine, coral and dark, are swept up in the force of it. They're up the stairs, through the doors into the lobby.

It is another world inside. It is stone sheen, gold, and gaslight. "Oh, Anna," Katherine says, and Anna presses her hand to her heart. Even then, even before she knows what will be stolen from her, even before she is aware of the possibility, Katherine wants every inch of this one birthday evening for keeps. She wants to lodge it deep, for all of time. She leads the way up the stairs and through the crowds and toward an arch and through a door and down the aisle toward their cushioned seats, holding Anna's hand. High above is the crystal chandelier, and Anna won't take her eyes off it; in Anna's eyes it shines. It's like the icicles that form on the edge of a roof when the sun gets trapped inside—a cascade of ice and sun.

"Like sitting inside a jewelry box," Anna whispers, and Katherine nods.

Everything is tiered. Everything is solid. The Corinthian columns at the proscenium. The private boxes at the theater's edge. The sapphire star in the hair of the woman seated directly ahead. For the moment it is forgotten that Adelina Patti has come to sing, that somewhere backstage she is transforming herself into Zerlina, but soon the curtain will rise. Soon. Though Katherine hopes that it will take forever.

That Katherine and Anna will belong, from now on, to all of this.

Katherine lifts her eyes to the balcony nearest the stage, along the east side of the Academy, which seems, like all the balconies, to float on air, like a bank of clouds in a gold and cranberry sky. The box is crowded with the well-dressed rich eager for Patti to take the stage—eight of them leaning and bending toward one another, two women with fans batting the air, one woman in black, the plainest woman Katherine has ever seen, even plainer than her mother.

Beside her sits a man with a straight back and a preoccupied aspect, as if he's come for obligation's sake but is somewhere else entirely in his head. He leans forward for a moment, rests his chin in one hand, and when he leans back, Katherine sees a woman, perhaps forty years old, looking grim and lifeless—immune, it seems, to the anticipatory chitter, the starlit chandelier, the stone sheen and jeweled gold, the curtain that will soon reveal all. She is stern, unyielding, while the conversation around her goes on, the batting of the air with oversize fans. It's as if the woman isn't really there at all, as if it is, in fact, a cloud she is on, a height she has ascended to on her own. A distance she has forged and holds to and must, Katherine thinks, be interfered with, broken.

Anna leans against Katherine and asks, "What are you staring at?"

"That woman. There. Do you see her?" Katherine gestures.

"Oh," Anna says, for she's Katherine's twin; she understands all.

"However does one grow so sad as that?"

"Or so old?" Anna says, and she shudders.

"She seems lonely, doesn't she? Seems like she's not really here."

"Don't let me get old," Anna says. "You have to promise."

Katherine turns and looks deep inside her sister's green eyes. "I promise you," she says.

And now the lights are going down, the curtain rising. Now all of those who have gathered here turn their attention to the stage. Now the flower in Anna's hair seems to open even broader, and Adelina Patti takes the stage.

"She's singing to me," Anna says. "Do you hear it?"

"She's singing to both of us," Katherine says.

Seventeen

THE BRIGADES ARE GONE. THE SHANTYTOWN FIRE has been beaten to the ground. The rescued exiles of the Centennial are crossing the widest bridge ever built, headed home. It is night, it is dark, the battle's over. The Schuylkill holds the reflections of the gas lamps on its back.

Over shoulders, between satchels, through the windows of passing carriages, Katherine strains to find him. Down the smoldering alleys that break south off of Elm, she turns. The investigators are already stomping about. The tavern owners are spent, dazed, culpable, gaunt. The fat lady lies in a heap beside the still-standing Titusville well, as if waiting for someone to sign her up for a new show. The guests of the Globe and the Trans-Continental are pacing the streets, confused and undecided, their best worldly goods in their hands. A cook runs about with a silver bowl inverted like a hat upon his head. But where is William, and his mutt?

The end of the day has become the certainty of night. The stink of the dead fire is overwhelming. Katherine has circled around, has circled back. Someone calls to her and asks if she is all right, but she doesn't dare to answer. For right then, from a distance down Belmont, Katherine hears the barking of a dog, and something tells her—a hunch—that it's that mutt. Lifting her skirts to her knees, she runs—past the Globe toward Operti's, where there is no music in the air, only the evening's aftermath, the *sizzle-pop*.

The moon is high and lights her way. The sound of the mutt draws nearer. Katherine hears the *thwack* and *thwack* of the mutt's sooted tail, and sees the dog at last. Now she looks past it, toward Operti's, which has miraculously escaped the wrath of the fire. On Operti's steps sits the girl—her gold cage in her hand, empty.

"Honey," Katherine calls to her, breathless. "Honey, what happened?"

"I can't find my bird," the girl cries out.

Katherine throws her arms around the child and sits. She presses her cheek against the child's cheek, trying to assess the situation, to imagine where the child's father has gone, how an entire orchestra has vanished. The fire began before Signor Giuseppe Operti could have ever lifted his baton. But where are the musicians? And where is the bird? And where is William?

"Birds fly," Katherine tells the child. "I'm sure your Snow is all right. Safe somewhere in a tree."

But the girl can no longer hold back her tears. She crumbles inside Katherine's arms, buries her head in Katherine's shoulder. She lets the gold cage topple onto the ground, and the mutt, hearing the clatter, comes closer, barks again.

"Snow's my best friend," the child murmurs.

"I understand," Katherine says.

They sit in the dark on those steps, and the mutt barks and chases its tail. Katherine is sure the child's father is out there, looking for his girl—panicked, too, over what seems lost, over all that will always be lost until and unless it is finally found. Katherine remembers the day on the river, the sight of Bennett sprawled out, plunging his hand through the portal of ice. He would have gone in after Anna. They wouldn't let him. He's lived with that. She must forgive him. She must forgive herself.

"What if Snow doesn't come back?" the child asks, and Katherine says, "Then you will always have Snow in your heart," and now the child sobs harder, and Katherine, too, allows her own tears to fall. Anna in her heart, she thinks. Katherine living, staying alive, so that Anna lives within.

Just then, the mutt turns, moans, stretches low—reaches its filthy front paws toward the shadows of Belmont's opposite side. The ears shoot up straight on its shaggy head, and Katherine looks to where the dog is looking, waits for the shadows across the way to break. Then the mutt leaps forward and William appears—his hands held out before him and clasped, as if he is holding a globe. He stops when he sees Katherine, takes a long step back. The mutt jumps high, pushes his paws against William's chest. "Get down now, boy," the young man says, but says it gently. "Fragile, boy," he warns. "Back down."

"Darling," Katherine says to the child. "Look up." For she knows at once what William has found; she hears the sound of the bird singing.

"Found her huddled on a window ledge," William says at last, looking up, catching Katherine's eyes with his own, which are the color of a river at night. "Took her a little time to decide to trust my hands," he says.

Katherine feels the warm weight of the child peel from her—sees her running down across Operti's steps. "Snow!" the child says, and William opens his hands slowly—reveals the undiminished whiteness of wings.

"Down, boy," William cautions the mutt. "Down, boy. Let the bird be." And now he transfers the bird to the girl's open hands, and the bird spreads its glamorous wings; it settles. The child leans in close toward her bird, and gives it a kiss on the beak.

"You've come home, Snow," she says. "You really have." She is astonished and grateful and hasn't got the words to express either feeling.

"Thank you," Katherine says for them both.

"William," he says, introducing himself.

"Katherine," she says. "We've met before."

"Of course we have. I remember."

She doesn't have to say when, or apologize for it. She

doesn't have to explain, though someday she will. Someday when she and William are walking by the river, she will tell him her whole story. She'll unspool the memories that she has of Anna—all of them, an entire life of them. But not yet. Not now.

"Quite the day at the Centennial," William says into the silence.

"An accident," she tells him. "All of it."

Katherine lifts the cage from the ground and carries it to the girl, holds the gold door open. Carefully, the child delivers Snow onto its roost. She closes the bird in, then looks up again to Katherine. "My father," she says, "will be worried."

"We'll take you home, then," Katherine says, offering the child a hand. To William then she offers her other.

He bows a little, as if accepting a dance. He smooths his wheat-colored hair, his borrowed trousers, which have charred, Katherine notices, with the fire. He settles his shoulders like a gentleman and yields his hand to Katherine's.

"There's the start of a breeze," she says, and she stands a little straighter, holds William's hand a little tighter, so that she might, for all of time, remember this.

Sources

Late-nineteenth-century Philadelphia is, for me, a place of endless fascinations. Among the many sources that I turned to throughout the writing of this book are the following: *The Illustrated History of the Centennial Exhibition: Philadelphia 1876: A Collector's Reprint* (James D. McCabe); *Within These Walls: A History of the Academy of Music in Philadelphia* (John Francis Marion); *Dressed for the Photographer: Ordinary Americans and Fashion, 1840–1900* (Joan Severa); *Designing the Centennial: A History of the 1876 International Exhibition in Philadelphia* (Bruno Giberti); *Forgotten Philadelphia: Lost Architecture of the Quaker City* (Thomas H. Keels); *A Century After: Picturesque Glimpses of Philadelphia and Pennsylvania* (Edward Strahan); *A Book of Remembrance* (Elizabeth Duane Gillespie); *What Ben Beverly Saw at the Great Exposition: A Souvenir of the Centennial, by a Chicago Lawyer* (John T. Dale); *Tommy's Folly: Through Fires, Hurricanes, and War, the Story of Congress Hall, Cape May, America's Oldest Seaside Hotel* (Jack Wright); *Preschool Education in America: The Culture of Young Children from the Colonial Era to the Present* (Barbara Beatty); *Images of America: Center City Philadelphia in the 19th Century*

(The Print and Photograph Department of the Library Company of Philadelphia); *Images of America: Philadelphia's 1876 Centennial Exhibition* (Linda P. Gross and Theresa R. Snyder); "Declaration of Rights of the Women of the United States by the National Woman Suffrage Association, July 4th, 1876" (The Elizabeth Cady Stanton and Susan B. Anthony Papers Project); "A Sennight of the Centennial," *Atlantic Monthly*, July 1876 (William Dean Howells); "In and About the Fair," *Scribner's Monthly*, September 1876 (Donald G. Mitchell); *Visitor's Guide to the Centennial Exhibition and Philadelphia: The Only Guide-Book Sold on the Exhibition Grounds* (J. B. Lippincott & Co.); Free Library of Philadelphia *The Centennial Exhibition Digital Collection* (http://libwww.library.phila.gov/CenCol); Free Library of Philadelphia Centennial Scrapbook (Print and Pictures Collection); *Digital History: Centennial Exposition, Philadelphia, 1876* (http://www.digitalhistory.uh.edu/learning_history/worlds_fair/centennial_resources.cfm); *The New York Times* (assorted Centennial articles); *Public Ledger* (assorted Centennial articles); and *The New Century for Women* (assorted Centennial articles).

Throughout the writing, I have held as true as possible to the facts. I did, however, take liberties with Adelina Patti, the celebrity soprano, who sang at the Academy on many occasions between December 1859 and November 1903. She was not, however, in town during the evening described here.

End Notes

On May 10, 1876, the one hundredth anniversary of the founding of the nation was celebrated by the Centennial Exhibition—a World's Fair of unprecedented proportion that brought upwards of 10 million people to fairgrounds just west of central Philadelphia during a six-month period. With exhibits on display from thirty-seven nations, with exotic plants blooming in Horticultural Hall and the ghost of George Washington rising from water fountains and coins, the Centennial signaled, most of all, the mounting preeminence of American technology.

Visitors from around the world gawked at such oddities as the typewriter and telephone, a lunch warmer, a stocking darner, a Pullman palace car, a stool with wheels designed for ambulating infants. They honored an eagle by the name of Old Abe who had been a mascot of a Wisconsin regiment in the Civil War. They were awed. And every day, without fail, the fourteen churring acres of time-saving machines in Machinery Hall were powered into action by the Double Corliss, a vertical engine of colossal proportions that was described by one observer as "an athlete of steel and iron," and which drew the close attention of Walt Whitman, who was found sitting at its feet.

Directly across the street from the Centennial stood Shantytown, where entertainment of another sort went down in taverns, alleys, and back rooms, and where, one discontented visitor avowed, one couldn't move "without unpleasant elbowing from low forms of vice, and contemplation of the worst forms of suburban ugliness." Brick kilns and tented saloons. Salacious dens and clapboard shells. Sea cows and educated pigs, gymnasts and prostitutes, intrigue and ale, always ale: this was the place.

It was during the course of my research for *Flow: The Life and Times of Philadelphia's Schuylkill River* that I began to dream, novelistically, about this Centennial year. About twin sisters and a boy who rescued animals. About a mother so preoccupied with the future that she could not see, or protect, the present. About a river with a mind of her own.

Stories like this one go through countless iterations. They require, above all else, a gritty faith. I needed others to keep me going. Among those dear souls are Ivy Goodman, Kate Moses, Rahna Reiko Rizzuto, Buzz Bissinger, Elizabeth Mosier, Alyson Hagy, Jennie Nash, Jan Shaeffer, Jane Satterfield, Anna Lefler, Adam Levine, Kate Wilhelm, Liz Rosenberg, Mandy Stanley, Vivian Mahoney, Melissa Walker, Sherry McIntosh, the brave librarians of both

Radnor Memorial Library and Free Library of Philadelphia, and Lori Salganicoff.

My agent, Amy Rennert, and her assistant, Robyn Russell, were trusted readers of early drafts, smart provocateurs, and most essential enthusiasts. My father, Kep Kephart, listened to my stories and traveled with me, on a rainy day, to the Centennial grounds, while my husband, Bill, accompanied me through the streets of West Philadelphia on a day of sun. Jill Santopolo read this book twice and helped me think harder and better about what it could be. My son, Jeremy, gave me room to talk about structure and voice; he took an abiding interest; he loved me when I failed and when I didn't; he taught me, as he always does, something new about heart.

And then there is Laura Geringer, who invited me, one early spring day, to share this book with her. She read it almost at once. She wrote a letter to which I will always return, when things seem bleak or dark. Laura spoke with me, at great length, about my dreams. She brought *Dangerous Neighbors* to a stunning publishing house called Egmont USA, where the publisher, Elizabeth Law, took generous interest, where Greg Ferguson gracefully steered things through, where Nico Medina and Kathryn Hinds paid exquisite attention to every line and fact, where Mary Albi and Robert Guzman oversaw the marketing effort, and where the incredibly talented Neil Swaab was brought on board to design the (to my mind) exquisite cover. Laura launched my career in young adult novels, and she gave me *Dangerous Neighbors* as well—making it not just an infinitely better book, but one that I might hold in my hands. For many years, I dreamed of holding this book in my hands.

I am unspeakably grateful.

BETH KEPHART is the author of a dozen books, including the National Book Award finalist *A Slant of Sun*; the BookSense pick *Ghosts in the Garden*; the autobiography of Philadelphia's Schuylkill River, *Flow*; and the critically acclaimed novels for young adults *Undercover*, *House of Dance*, *Nothing But Ghosts*, and *The Heart Is Not a Size*. Beth Kephart's acclaimed short story "The Longest Distance" appears in the May 2009 HarperTeen anthology *No Such Thing As the Real World*. She is a winner of the Pennsylvania Council on the Arts fiction grant, a National Endowment for the Arts grant, a Leeway grant, a Pew Fellowships in the Arts grant, and the Speakeasy Poetry Prize, among other honors. Kephart's essays are frequently anthologized, she has judged numerous competitions, and she has taught workshops at many institutions, to all ages. Kephart teaches advanced nonfiction at the University of Pennsylvania and served as the inaugural readergirlz author in residence.

Please visit Beth's blog, www.beth-kephart.blogspot.com.